"Why are you pretending that you find me so interesting?"

He leaned in close and she felt his lips brush against her cheek as he spoke. "I'm not pretending."

She thought about putting her arms around his neck and pulling him into her bedroom. But then she pictured the morning after. The awkwardness because she'd hope it was a beginning not an ending. She'd done that god-awful dance once before…. Nate worked for her. Was supposed to be at White Caps for the whole summer. The last thing she wanted was to be reminded daily of another bad decision when it came to men.

She stared up into his eyes and tried to read the future in the flecks of green and gold.

Pulling back, she thought there was a damn fine line between self-preservation and cowardice. "I think it's best that we not take things any further."

He smiled slowly. "What's life without a little excitement?"

Dear Reader,

It's hot and sunny in my neck of the woods—in other words, perfect beach reading weather! And we at Silhouette Special Edition are thrilled to start off your month with the long-awaited new book in *New York Times* bestselling author Debbie Macomber's Navy series, *Navy Husband*. It features a single widowed mother; her naval-phobic sister, assigned to care for her niece while her sister is in the service; and a handsome lieutenant commander who won't take no for an answer! In this case, I definitely think you'll find this book worth the wait....

Next, we begin our new inline series, MOST LIKELY TO..., the story of a college reunion and the about-to-be-revealed secret that is going to change everyone's lives. In *The Homecoming Hero Returns* by Joan Elliott Pickart, a young man once poised for athletic stardom who chose marriage and fatherhood instead finds himself face-to-face with the road not taken. In Stella Bagwell's next book in her MEN OF THE WEST series, *Redwing's Lady*, a Native American deputy sheriff and a single mother learn they have more in common than they thought. *The Father Factor* by Lilian Darcy tells the story of the reunion between a hotshot big-city corporate lawyer who's about to discover the truth about his father—and a woman with a secret of her own. If you've ever bought a lottery ticket, wondering, if just once, it could be possible...be sure to grab *Ticket to Love* by Jen Safrey, in which a pizza waitress from Long Island is sure that if *she* isn't the lucky winner, it must be the handsome stranger in town. Last, new-to-Silhouette author Jessica Bird begins THE MOOREHOUSE LEGACY, a miniseries based on three siblings who own an upstate New York inn, with *Beauty and the Black Sheep*. In it, responsible sister Frankie Moorehouse wonders if just this once she could think of herself first as soon as she lays eyes on her temporary new chef.

So keep reading! And think of us as the dog days of August begin to set in....

Toodles,

Gail Chasan
Senior Editor

Please address questions and book requests to:
Silhouette Reader Service
U.S.: 3010 Walden Ave., P.O. Box 1325, Buffalo, NY 14269
Canadian: P.O. Box 609, Fort Erie, Ont. L2A 5X3

BEAUTY AND THE BLACK SHEEP
Jessica Bird

SPECIAL EDITION®
Published by Silhouette Books

America's Publisher of Contemporary Romance

To my mother, with love.
And thanks for moving around all those boxes of books!

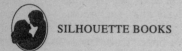 SILHOUETTE BOOKS

ISBN 0-373-24698-6

BEAUTY AND THE BLACK SHEEP

Copyright © 2005 by Jessica Bird

This edition published by arrangement with Harlequin Books S.A.

Visit Silhouette Books at www.eHarlequin.com

Printed in U.S.A.

JESSICA BIRD

graduated from college with a double major in history and art history, concentrating in the medieval period. This meant she was great at discussing anything that happened before the sixteenth century, but not all that employable in the real world. In order to support herself, she went to law school and worked in Boston in healthcare administration for many years.

She now lives in the South with her husband and many pictures of golden retrievers that she hopes to replace with the real thing sometime very soon. As a writer, her commute is a heck of a lot better than it was as a lawyer and she's thrilled that her professional wardrobe includes slippers and sweatpants. She likes to write love stories that feature strong, independent heroines and complex, alpha male heroes. Visit her Web site at www.jessicabird.com and e-mail her at Jessica@jessicabird.com.

Chapter One

The only warning Frankie Moorehouse had that twenty gallons of water were going to fall on her and her desk was a single drop.

One drop.

It hit the financial statement she was reviewing, right in the middle of the page that suggested the White Caps Bed & Breakfast was dangerously close to going under.

She groaned, figuring the roof must be leaking again. The sprawling mansion had all kinds of nooks and crannies, which made for an elegant and interesting floor plan. Unfortunately, the roof covering all of these architectural treasures was a complicated warren of angles that trapped old leaves and moisture, creating little pockets of rot.

Squinting her eyes, she glanced out the window, searching the dimming light for a rainstorm that wasn't there.

She looked up with a frown, saw a darkened spot on the ceiling, and had just enough time to get out the words "What the hell—" before the torrent hit her.

The water carried with it chunks of horse-hair plaster from the ceiling and an evil tide of filth that had collected in the rafters. It hit her in a stinky mess, splashing all over the desk and the floor in a great whoosh of noise. When the torrent ceased, she took her glasses off and lifted her arms, watching brown rivulets drip off her skin.

It smelled, she thought, like bat guano.

The sound of pounding footsteps heading her way was neither reassuring nor welcome. She shot up from the desk and shut the door to the office.

"Hey, Frankie, what happened?" George's booming voice sounded characteristically confused. He'd worked for her for about six weeks and sometimes the only difference she could find between him and an inanimate object was that occasionally he blinked.

In the kitchen that serviced the White Caps dining room, George was supposed to be the fry-guy, the *souschef,* the *pâtissier* and the busboy. What he did do was take up space. At six feet seven inches, and tilting the scale at well over three hundred pounds, he was a big oaf of a man. And she'd have fired him on day two except he had a good heart, he needed a job and a place to stay, and he was nice to Frankie's grandmother.

"Frankie, you okay?"

"I'm fine, George." Which was her standard reply to the question she despised. "You better go make sure the bread's cut for the baskets, okay?"

"Yeah, sure. Okay, Frankie."

She closed her eyes. The sound of dripping, dirty

water reminded her that not only did she have to pull off yet another magic trick to balance the account for the month, she had to clean up her office.

At least she had the Shop-Vac to use for the latter.

Much to her dismay, White Caps had financial problems she couldn't seem to solve no matter how hard she worked. Housed in the old Moorehouse mansion, on the shores of Saranac Lake in the Adirondack Mountains, the ten-bedroom B & B had been struggling for the past five years. People weren't traveling as much as they used to, so overnight guests were fewer and fewer and there wasn't enough local traffic in the dining room to cover the costs of the operation.

It wasn't just a general reduction in tourist trade that was the problem. The house itself was part of the reason the reservations were drying up. Once a gracious summer home from the Federal Period, it needed a major overhaul. Band-Aid fixes such as a fresh coat of paint or some pretty window boxes could no longer hide the fact that dry rot was eating up the porches, the eaves were rotting and the floors were beginning to bow.

And every year it was something else. Another part of the roof to fix. A boiler to be replaced.

She glared at the exposed pipes over her desk.

Plumbing that needed to be rehauled.

Frankie wadded up the spreadsheet and threw it in the trash, thinking she'd prefer to have been born into a family that had never had anything rather than one that had gradually lost everything.

And as she picked some of the plaster out of her hair, she decided the house wasn't the only thing getting older and less attractive.

At the age of thirty-one, she felt more like fifty-one. She'd been working seven days a week for a decade and couldn't remember when she'd last had her hair done or bought a new piece of clothing, other than work uniforms. Her fingernails were chewed to the quick, her hands shook all the time and her diet consisted of coffee, breadbasket leftovers and more coffee.

"Frankie?"

Her sister's voice was subdued as it came through the door and Frankie had to struggle not to scream back, *Don't ask me if I'm okay!*

"Are you okay?"

She squeezed her eye lids closed. "I'm fine, Joy."

There was a long silence. She imagined her sister leaning into the door, one pale hand against the wood, a worried expression on her perfectly beautiful, Pre-Raphaelite face.

"Joy, where's Grand-Em?" Frankie knew that asking about their grandmother, Emma, would channel the concern somewhere else.

"She's reading the telephone book."

Good. That was known to quiet the dementia at least for a little while.

In the pause that followed, Frankie stood up and started to grab hunks of plaster off the floor and the desk.

"Ah, Frankie?"

"Yes?"

The reply was so quiet, she stopped cleaning up and strained to hear Joy's voice through the wood panels. "Speak up, for God's sakes, I can't hear you."

"Ah, Chuck called."

Frankie pitched some plaster into the trash can, nearly knocking the thing over from the force.

"Don't tell me he's going to be late again. This is Friday of the Fourth of July weekend." Which meant with the way things had gone last season, they would probably have a couple of people come for dinner from town. With two sets of guests in the house, there could be nine or ten expecting food. The number was nothing like it used to be, but those people needed to be fed.

Joy's voice became muffled again so Frankie threw open the door. "What?"

Her sister took a quick step back, cornflower blue eyes stretching wide as Frankie brushed a wet length of brown hair out of her face.

"Don't say one word, Joy, unless it's about the message from Chuck. Not one word."

Her sister started talking fast and Frankie got the gist. Chuck and his girlfriend Melissa. Getting married. Moving to Las Vegas. Not coming in, tonight or ever.

Frankie sagged against the doorjamb, feeling her wet clothes and her apprehension cling to her like a second skin. When Joy reached out, Frankie shrugged off the concern and snapped to attention.

"Okay, first, I'm going to go take a shower and then here's what we're going do."

Lucille's life ended not with a whimper but a bang on a back road somewhere in the Adirondack Mountains of upstate New York.

Going seventy miles an hour, the 1987 SAAB 9000 blew a gasket and that was game over. With a burst of noise as loud as a gunshot, she relinquished her usefulness with protest and wheezed to a stop.

Nate Walker, her first and only owner, let out a curse.

When he tried the key, he wasn't surprised when the response came from the starter, not the engine.

"Aww, Lucy honey. Don't be like this." He caressed the steering wheel but knew damn well that begging wasn't going to fix whatever had made that kind of noise.

It was probably hydraulic lift time.

Opening the door, he got out and stretched. He'd been driving for four hours straight, heading from New York City to Montreal, but this was hardly the kind of break he had in mind. Eyeing the road, which was just a little asphalt and some yellow paint away from being a footpath, he figured his first move had to be getting Lucille out of the way of traffic.

Not that he had to rush. He'd seen one other car in the last twenty minutes. Looking around, there was only thick forest, more of the thin road and the gathering darkness. Silence pressed in on him.

Putting Lucille in Neutral, he braced his shoulder against the doorjamb and pushed, steering through the window with his right hand. When she was safely on the rough, scratchy grass at the side of the road, he popped the hood, got out his flashlight and gave her a look-see. As Lucille had aged, he'd gained a proficiency in auto repair, but a quick inspection told him he might be out of his league. There was smoke coming out of her and a hissing noise that suggested she was leaking something.

He shut the hood and leaned back against it, looking up at the sky.

Night was coming on fast, and being far to the north it was cool even in July. He didn't know how much walking it was going to take to reach the next town so he figured he better be prepared for a hike. Going around to the front seat, he threw on his battered leather jacket and collected some provisions. Stuffing the bottle of water he'd been nursing and the remnants of the turkey grinder he'd had for lunch into his backpack, he reckoned he had enough to last him.

Before locking up the car, he grabbed his knife roll. The heavy leather bundle, which was tied tightly with a strap, felt good in his hand. Inside were six pristine chef's knives made of carbon and stainless steel, and taking them with him was second nature. A chef's knives were never to be left unattended, even locked in a car on the side of the road in the middle of nowhere.

The rest of his crap he couldn't care less about, not that there was a lot of it. He had some clothes, all of them old, most of them repaired in one manner or another. Had two pairs of boots, also old and repaired. And he had Lucille. Who was old, and repaired but now not so usable.

His knives, however, were not only new, they were state of the art. And they were worth more than Lucille.

Which probably wasn't saying much anymore.

Kissing his palm, he laid it on Lucille's still warm hood and started out.

His boots made a heavy noise as they hit the asphalt and he settled the backpack comfortably on one shoulder. While walking along, he looked up at the sky. The stars were incredibly bright, particularly one dead center above him. The thing was flickering like a broken light and he started to think of it as a companion.

Mailboxes soon sprouted at the side of the road. Mailboxes and imposing stone gates. He figured he was getting close to one of the old-fashioned resort areas where the Victorian wealthy had once escaped the heat of New York and Philadelphia in the days before air-conditioning. The rich still came to the Adirondacks, of course, but now it was strictly for the area's rugged beauty rather than from a lack of Freon in their life.

He titled his head back to the sky.

Man, that star was *alive*. Maybe it wasn't even a star. Maybe it was a satellite, although then it would be moving—

Nate felt his boot tip and the next thing he knew he was ass over elbow, falling into a ditch. On his way to the ground, he made himself go limp as he prepared for a rough landing. Fortunately, the earth was soft, but a shooting pain in his lower leg told him he wasn't going to walk away from the fall without a limp.

He lay on his side for a minute. He couldn't see his star anymore from the new vantage point, although he had a good shot at the ravine he'd almost rolled into. He sat up, brushed some leaves off his jacket and felt okay. When he got to his feet and tried to put weight on his left leg, however, his ankle let out a howl of protest.

Great. Out in the middle of nowhere. Car dead at the side of the road. And a mission-critical body part that was not passive aggressive in its opinions.

Nate grit his teeth and started walking. He knew he wasn't going to make it farther than a quarter mile on the ankle. And that was if he had crutches.

The next mailbox, the next driveway, the next car was going to be it for him. He needed a phone and maybe a place to spend the night. By morning, he figured his ankle would feel better and he'd be able to get Lucille going somehow.

Hobbling along, pain shooting up his calf and down

into his foot, Nate thought this was not exactly where he'd planned for his drive to take him.

Frankie caught the burning smell first and raced for the oven. She'd been so distracted trying to clean pears for poaching that she'd forgotten all about the chicken she'd put in to cook.

When she opened the oven door, smoke poured out and she grabbed two folded side towels for the evacuation. Holding the roasting pan away from her body, as if the thing was radioactive, she threw it down on the counter.

The sound of a pot on the stove boiling over drowned out most of her curses.

"That don't look right," George said.

Frankie let her head fall forward, trying to keep from cursing again. The temptation was nearly irresistible, especially when he followed up with, "Maybe you should try that one more time."

Joy rushed into the kitchen from the dining room in mid-sentence. "The Littles, that couple whose bureau wouldn't open when they went to unpack, they want their dinner now. They've been waiting for forty-five minutes and—oh."

Frankie took a deep breath. Even if the Littles hadn't been rude as hell about the bureau, the lumpy pillows on the bed, the cleanliness of the windows and the fact there were wire hangers in the closet, she didn't see how she could serve them the desecrated carcass.

But now what? If White Caps was closer to civilization, she would have called for take-out from some other restaurant in the first place rather than take a chance on her cooking skills. Deep in the Adirondacks, though, the closest food emporium with anything ready to eat was the Bait Shoppe.

Although feeding the Littles night crawlers disguised as gourmet cuisine had some appeal.

"What are we going to do?" Joy asked.

Frankie reached over to turn off the oven and saw that she'd put the thing on broil, not bake. Of all the stupid mistakes...

"Frankie?"

She could feel Joy and George staring at her and to avoid their eyes, she looked down at the chicken. Her mind went blank. She was aware of a humming in her ears and that was about it. Except for her feet. She could feel them pounding inside the ancient running shoes she had on, as if someone had a vise to her toes.

How old were those shoes, she wondered idly. Five years?

"Frankie?"

She looked up at her sister whose face was wide open. Joy was ready for direction. Ready to be saved.

God, what she wouldn't give to be able to look at someone with that kind of expectant hope.

"Yeah, okay," she murmured. "Let me think."

Like a tired lawnmower, her brain started to churn again. Options, they needed options. What else was in the meat locker? Only big cuts. And the freezer—no, there was no time to defrost anything. Leftovers. What could she bash together out of—

The sound of someone pounding on the back door brought her head around.

Joy looked to the noise and then back at her.

"Answer it," Frankie said, heading for the walk-in refrigerator. "George, take the Littles more bread."

She was searching the shelves and seeing nothing that offered a solution when her sister let out a startled *hello*.

Frankie looked over her shoulder and lost her train of thought.

A man the size of a barn had walked into the White Caps kitchen.

God, he was as big as George, although not built the same. Definitely not built like George. This guy was hefty where you wanted a man to be: in the shoulders, in the arms. Not in the stomach.

And he was almost too handsome to look at. Wearing a black leather jacket and carrying a beat-up backpack on one shoulder, he looked like a drifter but carried himself as if he knew exactly where he was. He had thick dark hair that was on the long side and his face was stunning, though it seemed as if it belonged on someone else. His features were a little too patrician to be attached to a man dressed the way he was.

But his eyes—his eyes were what really stood out. They were extraordinary—dark as the night, deep set, with thick lashes.

And they were totally focused on her sister.

Given how slight she was, Joy looked like a child standing in front of him with her head tilted up. And Frankie knew exactly the kind of resplendent astonishment that would be showing on her sister's face, so it was no wonder the man looked poleaxed. Any guy worth his testosterone would be snared by that expression alone, much less the fact that it was shining out of such a garden of female delights.

Great. Just what she needed, some tourist lost and looking for directions. Or worse, a wanderer looking for work. She could barely keep Joy and George on the straight and narrow. The last thing she needed was another big lug kicking around.

"Hey there, Angel," the man said. A bemused expression was tinting his handsome features as if he'd never seen anything like the girl standing in front of him.

"My name is Joy, actually." Even though Frankie couldn't see it, she heard the smile on her sister's face.

Flattening her lips, Frankie decided it was time to get involved. Before the stranger melted onto the damn floor.

"Can we help you?" she said sharply.

The man frowned, looked over at her and the force of those eyes hit her like a gust of wind. She swallowed through a tight throat. There was nothing dim-witted or slow about him, she realized. He was downright shrewd as he scanned her from head to foot.

As a flush came up into her face, she reminded herself that she had dinner to get ready, a staff, such as it was, to motivate, a business to run. Unlike her little sister, she didn't have the luxury of staring up into some man's face for days on end.

Although, jeez, what a face that was.

"Well?" she said.

"My car broke down about two miles back." He gestured over one shoulder. "I need to use a phone."

So he was headed through town. Good.

"There's one back in my office. I'll show you the way." She shut the door to the walk-in.

"Thanks." As he stepped forward, he sniffed and grimaced. When he caught sight of the desecrated chicken, he laughed. "So your chef moonlights as an arsonist? Or is it the other way around?"

Frankie found herself measuring his carotid artery and thinking things that could lead to her arrest. While he was making fun of her failure, he was wasting time she didn't have to spare.

She was holding herself in check and about to lead him out of the kitchen when the door from the dining room swung open. George came back with a full bread-basket in his hand, looking like he was on the verge of tears.

"They're hungry. Really hungry, Frankie," he said, staring down at his shoes. "And the Littles don't want any more bread."

She tightened her lips in a grim line again. Considering what those two entitled big mouths had tried to do to her over the various inadequacies of their room, she could only imagine what they'd done to George.

Which was totally unfair, she thought. The poor man didn't deserve to be the salad course. It wasn't his fault she'd burned the entrée.

"I tried to tell them it wouldn't be long," he said.

"I know, George. I know. Why don't you go get a cookie, okay?" She went over and stared at the chicken, willing it into edible condition while George put the basket down and headed for the pantry.

She picked up a knife and thought she could salvage something. Cut off the black skin, maybe. But then what?

She heard a thud and realized that the stranger had thrown his backpack down on the stainless steel island next to her. Next, he tore off his jacket and tossed it across the room where it landed beautifully on a chair.

Frankie glanced over at the faded black T-shirt he was wearing. It was tight on him, leaving little to the imagination. To get away from the view of his chest, she looked up, way up. His eyes weren't black after all, they were hazel. Dark green with flecks of yellow.

And they were incredibly attractive, she thought. Could probably melt paint off a car door if they looked at you with passion.

She shook her head to clear it and then wondered why he was crowding her space.

"Excuse me," she said, holding her ground. "The phone's through that door and take a right into the office. Oh, and don't mind the water."

The man frowned. And then nudged her out of the way until he was standing in front of the chicken.

She was too dumbfounded to respond as he reached into the pack and pulled out a leather package. With a deft flip of the hand, it unrolled to reveal half a dozen knives that gleamed.

Frankie jumped back, thinking she might be the one who needed the phone. To call the police.

"How many?" he said in a voice like a drill sergeant.

"I beg your—"

His eyes were sharp, his tone bored. "How. Many."

Frankie was aware that no one in the room was moving. Joy was frozen to the spot near the dining room door, George had stopped with the cookie halfway on a return trip to his mouth. They were obviously waiting for her to explode.

She looked at the chicken and then back at the man who by now had picked up a long knife and was poised over the carcass. With that tool in his hand, he was all business.

"You're a cook?" she asked.

"No, a blacksmith."

As she stared up at him, the challenge in those hazel eyes was as clear as the bind she was in.

She had a choice. Rely on her skills, which had already resulted in the incineration of a sizable hunk of protein. Or take a gamble on this stranger and his flashy set of knives.

"Two parties of two. One six top," she said briskly.

"Okay, here's what I'm going to need." He looked over at her sister and when he spoke next, his voice was back to being gentle. "Angel, honey, I need you to take one of those pots over there and put it on the gas with two cups of water in it."

Joy leaped into service.

"George, is that your name?" the man asked. George nodded, happier now that the tension had dispersed and his cookie was finished. "I want you to pick up that head of lettuce and run it under the cold water, stroking each leaf like it was a cat. You got it?"

George beamed and started on his job. By this time, Joy had filled the pot and put it on a burner.

The stranger started in with the chicken, peeling off the skin with deft movements of his fingers and the knife. He worked with such speed and confidence, she was momentarily captivated.

"Now, Angel—" back with the soft voice "—I want you to bring me a pound of butter, some cream, three eggs and all the curry powder you can find. And do you have any frozen vegetables?"

Frankie cut in, feeling ignored. "We've got fresh Brussels sprouts, broccoli—"

"Angel, I need something small. Peas? Cubed carrots?"

"We've got corn, I think," Joy said enthusiastically.

"Good. Bring it over and get some twine."

Frankie stepped back, feeling more panicked now

than when things were disorganized and she had no options.

She should be doing something, she thought.

George came back with the lettuce and Frankie was impressed. Chuck, the former cook, had never been able to get him to do anything right, but here he was with perfectly cleaned romaine leaves.

"Good job, George, that's perfect." The stranger handed George a knife. "Now cut it up in strips as wide as your thumb. But *do not* use your thumb to measure. It doesn't have to be exact. Do it across from me so I can watch you, okay?"

Joy came up to him with the bag of corn and the twine. She was smiling, so eager to please. "Do I put the corn in the water?"

"No." He lifted his left leg. "Tie it on to my ankle. The damn thing's killing me."

Chapter Two

Less than ten minutes later, Frankie took out the salads. They had a dressing on them that the man had whipped up out of some spices, olive oil and lemon juice. George, bless his heart, had cut up the crisp lettuce perfectly and had triumphed with the strips of red, yellow and orange peppers as well.

By this time, the local diners had left because they had perfectly good kitchens of their own to go home to, but the B & B's guests were like zoo animals they were so hungry. She had no idea what the stuff tasted like, but figured the Littles and the other couple were so hypoglycemic they probably wouldn't have cared if she'd served them dog food.

After she put the plates down in front of them, the Littles glared at her as they stabbed at the salad.

"Glad you finally got around to it," Mr. Little

snapped. "What were you doing, growing the leaves back there?"

She gave him and his anemic, stressed-out wife a frozen smile, glad she hadn't sent George or Joy out. She was bolting back for the kitchen when she heard the man say, "My God. This is…edible."

Great, Chef Wonderful got the raw veggies right. But what about the chicken?

As she pushed through the kitchen door, she wondered why she was being so critical of a guy who seemed to be saving her bacon, but she didn't dwell on the thought. She was too astonished at the sight of George laying out a row of his favorite oatmeal and raisin cookies on a sheet of cheesecloth.

The stranger was talking, in that calm voice.

"And then you're going to hold them over the boiling water when we're ready. Okay, Georgie?" he was saying. "So they get soft."

All Frankie could do was watch in amazement as the man, in a whirling dervish of motion, created dinner out of disaster. Twenty minutes later, he was spooning onto White Caps plates a curried, creamed chicken mixture that smelled out of this world.

"Now, it's your turn, Angel. Come on, follow me."

As he worked his way down a row of four plates, Joy was right behind him, sprinkling on raisins and almonds. Then the man packed couscous into a series of coffee cups and tapped out the mounds onto each plate. A sprig of parsley was put on top and then the man called, "Pick up."

Frankie sprang into action, scooping up the plates at once, as she'd done since she started waiting tables when she was a teenager.

"Joy, you clear," she called out.

Joy swept into the dining room with her, clearing the salads as Frankie slid the entrées in place.

It was over two hours later. Against all odds, the guests left happy and raving about the food, even the godforsaken Littles. The kitchen was cleaned up. And Joy and George were positively glowing with the good job they'd done under the stranger's direction.

Frankie was the only one out of sorts.

She should have been falling on her knees to thank the man with the fancy knives and the quick hands. She should have been delirious with relief. Instead, she was crabby. Having always been the savior, it was hard to accept a demotion in favor of a man she didn't know, who'd come out of nowhere.

And who still had a bag of frozen corn tied to his ankle.

The cook finished wiping off one of his knives and leaned under the overhead track lights to examine the blade carefully. Apparently satisfied with what he saw, he slid it into the leather roll and tied up the bundle. When he put it into the backpack, she realized he'd never gotten to make his call.

"You want to use the phone now?" Her voice was gruff because what she needed to do was thank him, but gratitude was something she was rusty with. She was used to giving orders, not praising initiative, and the role reversal felt uncomfortable.

And maybe she was just a little envious of how easily he'd pulled everything together.

Which was a perfectly ridiculous way to feel.

When he looked at her, his eyes narrowed. Considering how relaxed he was with Joy and George, Frankie figured he must not like her very much. The idea irked her even though she knew there was no reason to care what his opinion of her was. She wasn't going to see him again. Didn't even know his name, as a matter of fact.

Instead of answering her, he looked over at Joy who had one foot on the stairs that led to the servants' quarters. "Good night, Angel. You did a really good job tonight."

Frankie wondered how he'd known that Joy was yawning and about to disappear up to bed when he'd been focusing on his knives.

Joy's charming smile flashed across the kitchen. "Thanks, Nate."

And that was how Frankie learned his name.

Nate zipped his pack closed and regarded the woman staring up at him evenly.

Behind her vague hostility, he could see exhaustion lurking. She looked worn down and had the drooping mouth of someone who had barked too many orders to too many people in an enterprise that was going under.

He'd met a lot of managers just like her over the years.

Failure was everywhere around the White Caps Bed & Breakfast. From what he'd seen outside, in the kitchen and through one quick look into the dining room, the place was a ball gown with sweat stains, a once beautiful mansion on the long fade into a junk pile.

And the business was taking this woman down with it.

How old was she? Early thirties? She probably looked older than she was and he tried to imagine what was under the long bangs and sensible glasses, the loose white waitstaff shirt and standard issue black pants.

She'd probably been full of hope when she'd bought the old ark and he imagined that optimism had lasted only until it became clear that servicing rich weekenders was a thankless job, a low-praise zone in the extreme. And then the first fix-it bill had probably come for a boiler or a roof or major piece of equipment, giving her a sense of how much old charm cost.

As if on cue, a wheeze came out of the walk-in. The noise was followed by something close to a cough, like there was a little old man dying in the compressor.

He watched while she closed her eyes as if deliberately ignoring the sounds.

If Nate was a betting man, he'd guess in one year White Caps would either be under new management or condemned by the state.

Her eyes flipped open. "So. The phone?"

She was definitely a fighter, though. Tough as nails, maybe even prepared to go down with the ship, although where that trip would take her he couldn't imagine. More debt? Less sleep?

Or maybe she was just tending the pile of wood for her husband. Nate eyed her ring finger and didn't see anything on it.

"Hello? Nate? Or whatever you call yourself. Use the phone or move out. It's closing time."

"Okay. Thanks," he said, turning around and heading in the direction she'd pointed to earlier that evening. He walked into a darkened office and frowned when his feet made a sloppy noise, as if there were water on the floor.

He hit the light switch.

Good Lord, the place was soaked. He looked up at the ceiling, seeing a gaping hole that exposed pipes old enough to have been laid by God Himself.

Shaking his head, he reached for the phone, thinking he'd be lucky to get a dial tone. When he did, he punched in his buddy Spike's cell phone number. He and Spike had been friends since they'd gone through the Culinary Institute of America as classmates and they'd decided to buy a restaurant together. Their business interest was behind Nate's trip. After four months of searching, they couldn't seem to find what they wanted in their price range in Manhattan so they were looking at other cities. Spike had found a place for them to consider in Montreal, but Nate wasn't getting his hopes up. He didn't think the situation was going to be any better over the border in Canada.

He absolutely believed they could make it as owners. Between his skills at the stove and Spike's masterful work with pastries and breads, they had the fundamentals covered. But money was growing tight. Because Nate was living off the savings he was going to put toward their down payment, he was thinking it might be time to get a job for the summer and suspend the search at least until the fall. By then, new prospects would surely be on the market.

When he hung up with Spike, he looked toward the woman waiting in the doorway.

"What happened to your cook?" he asked.

"He quit tonight."

Nate nodded, thinking that was the way of the kitchen world. You never got tenure as a chef but the trade-off was you didn't have to give notice.

She began to tap her foot impatiently, but he wasn't in a hurry. Taking a look around he saw a desk, a computer, a couple of chairs, some closet doors. There was nothing particularly interesting about the room until he got to the bookcases. To her left, he saw an old photograph of a young family smiling into the camera. Two parents, three children, clothes from the seventies.

He went over for a closer look but when he picked it up off the shelf, she snatched the frame out of his hand.

"Do you mind?"

They were standing close and he became curiously aware of her. In spite of the bangs and the Poindexter glasses, the baggy clothes and the bags under her eyes, his body started to heat up. Her eyes widened and he wondered if she felt it, too—the odd current that seemed to run between them.

"You looking for someone in your kitchen?" he asked abruptly.

"I don't know," she said, clipping the words short.

"You sure needed someone tonight. You'd have been up the creek if I hadn't walked through your door."

"How about this, I don't know if I need *you*." She put the photograph back, laying it face down on the shelf.

"You think I'm not qualified?" He smiled when she remained silent, figuring she probably hated the fact that he'd saved her. "Tell me, just how did I fail to impress you tonight?"

"You did fine but that doesn't mean I'm going to hire you."

He shook his head. "Fine? Man, you have a hard time with compliments, don't you?"

"I don't waste energy playing spit and polish with egos. Especially healthy ones."

"So you prefer being around the depressed?" he retorted mildly.

"What's that supposed to mean?"

Nate shrugged. "Your staff's so beaten down it's a wonder they can put one foot in front of the other. That poor girl was ready to work herself to death tonight just for a kind word and George soaked up a little praise like he hadn't heard any in a month."

"Who made you an expert on those two?" Her hands were on her hips now as she looked up at him.

"It's just obvious, lady. If you took your blinders off once in a while you might see what you're doing to them."

"What *I'm* doing to them? I'll tell you what I'm doing to them." She jabbed a finger at him. "I'm keeping a roof over Joy's head and George out of a group home. So you can back off with the judgments."

As she glared at him, he wondered why he was arguing with her. The last thing the woman needed was another battle. Besides, why did he care?

"Look, ah—why don't we start over," he said. "Can we call a truce here?"

He stuck his hand out, aware that he'd just decided to take a job he wasn't being offered. But hell, he needed to spend the summer somewhere and she clearly needed the help. And White Caps was as good as any other place, even if it was sinking. At least he could have some fun and try out some new things he'd been thinking of without the food critics chomping at him.

When she just stared at him, he prompted her by looking down at his hand.

She tucked her arms into her body. "I think you better go."

"Are you always this unreasonable?"

"Good night."

He dropped his hand. "Let me get this straight. You have no cook. You're looking at one who's willing to work. But you'd rather shoot yourself in the foot just because you don't like me?" When she kept looking at him, buttoned up tight, he shook his head. "Damn, woman. You ever think this place might be going under because of you?"

The strained silence that followed was the calm before the storm. He knew it because she started to shake and he had a vague thought that he should duck.

But what came at him wasn't angry words or a slap or a right hook.

She started to cry. From behind the lenses, he saw tears well and then fall.

"Oh, God," he pushed a hand through his hair. "I didn't mean—"

"You don't know me," she said hoarsely and, somehow, regally. Even through her tears, she faced him squarely as if she had nothing to hide, as if the crying jag was a temporary aberration, nothing that spelled the end of her inner strength. "You don't know what's going on here. You don't—don't know what we've been through. So you can just put your pack on and start walking."

He reached out for her, not sure what he would do. Not take her in his arms, certainly. But he had some vague idea he could…pat her on the shoulder. Or something.

God, how lame was that.

Nate wasn't at all surprised when she shrugged him off and left him alone in her wet mess of an office.

In the pantry, surrounded by canned vegetables, bags of George's cookies and jars full of condiments, Frankie pulled herself together. Wiping her eyes with the palms of her hands, she sniffled a couple of times and then tugged her shirt into place.

She couldn't believe she'd cracked like that. In front of some stranger.

It was better than crying in front of Joy, sure, but not by much.

Boy, he'd nailed her vulnerable point. The idea that White Caps was failing because of her was her biggest fear and the mere thought of it was enough to make her start tearing up all over again.

God, what was she going to tell Joy if they had to leave? Where would they live? And how could she earn enough to take care of both her sister and Grand-Em?

What would she tell Alex?

She closed her eyes and leaned back against the shelves.

Alex.

She wondered where her brother was. Last she'd heard from him, he'd been training for the America's Cup off the Bahamas, but that had been back in February. As a competitive sailor, he traveled all over the world, and tracking his movements would have required a good map and a lot of patience.

Neither of which she had.

Considering the terrible events on the lake, which had left the three of them orphans when Frankie had just turned twenty-two, the fact that Alex lived on the sea was a perennial source of heartache. Like all families of sailors, however, she'd learned to live with the fear and work around it.

You can do a lot of things if you have to, she thought.

She'd turned into Wonder Woman thanks to getting trapped by fate.

An overworked, cranky Wonder Woman maybe, but she was still doing it all.

Frankie took a deep breath thinking, just once, she'd like to share the load. Have someone else make a decision. Take a direction. Lead.

She felt her shoulders sinking toward the floor as she tried to imagine Joy doing anything other than float around. George knew when he needed to eat and when it was time to sleep and not much else. Grand-Em thought it was still 1953.

But then, with the vividness of a movie clip, she had a vision of Nate's hands flying around the chicken she'd burned.

He was right. She did need a cook and he was, evidently, available.

And the man was good, she thought.

There was also the reality that there wasn't a long line of people applying for the job.

Wheeling around, Frankie burst out of the pantry, prepared to run after him, but she jerked to a halt. He'd been waiting, leaning casually against the island.

"I didn't want to leave until I knew you were okay," he explained.

"Do you want the job?"

He cocked an eyebrow, apparently unfazed by her turnaround. "Yeah. I'll stay until Labor Day."

"I can't pay you much, but then again, there won't be much you'll have to do."

He shrugged. "Money's not important to me."

At least he had one good trait, she thought, naming what sounded like a pathetically small salary.

"And I can offer you room and board." She straightened her shoulders. "But I want to be clear about something."

"Let me guess, you're the boss."

"Well, yes. More importantly, stay away from my sister."

He frowned. "Angel?"

"Her name is Joy. And she's not interested."

His laugh was short. "Don't you think that should be her choice, not yours?"

"No, I don't. Do we understand each other?"

A small smile played over his lips, but she couldn't divine what he thought was so amusing.

"Well?" she demanded.

"Yeah, I understand you perfectly." He extended his hand and raised that brow again. "You going to touch me this time?"

It was a taunt, a challenge.

And Frankie never backed down from anything.

She grabbed his hand like it was a door handle, in a tough grip meant to tell him that she was all business. But at the contact, she lost her pretensions. A shiver of awareness prickled across every square inch of her body and all she could do was blink up at him in confusion.

His eyes narrowed, the lids falling down over that fascinating spectrum of color. She felt him squeeze her hand and had a ludicrous image of him pulling her forward so he could kiss her.

God, what he could do to her, she thought, if they were naked and in a bed together—

Frankie stepped back quickly, thinking maybe she needed to get hit with some more water.

"Remember what I said," she ground out. "Don't go near my sister."

He scratched the side of his neck casually and put his hands into his pockets. She had a feeling that he didn't take orders well, but couldn't have cared less. He was working for her, which meant she called the shots. Period. End of story.

And the last thing Frankie needed to worry about was Joy getting her heart broken. Or being left pregnant and alone at the end of the summer. God knew, they couldn't afford another dependent.

"We're clear?" she prompted.

He didn't answer but she knew he understood her by the way his jaw was locked.

"Then I'll show you to your room." She walked around, flipping off lights, then headed for the back stairs.

When the Moorehouses had been rich, before generations of dandies enjoying the good life had drained the bank accounts and caused the stocks, jewelry and the best of the art to be sold off, the family had stayed in the big bedrooms in the front of the house that faced the lake. Now that they were the servants, they stayed where a fleet of maids and butlers had once slept. The staff wing, which stretched behind the mansion, had low ceilings, pine floors and no ornamentation. It was hot in the summer, drafty in the winter and the plumbing groaned.

Well, that last one was actually happening in the rest of the house by now, too.

At the head of the stairs, the corridor went off in both directions and there was no question where the new cook was going to sleep. Frankie didn't relish the idea of him being close to her, but at least if he was she could keep an eye on him. She headed left, taking them away from Joy's room.

As Frankie pushed open a door, she figured he'd be untroubled by the sparse accommodations. He looked as if he might have slept in cars and on park benches on occasion, so a bed was no doubt luxury enough.

"I'll go get your sheets," she said. "You and I are sharing a bathroom. It's right next door."

She went to the linen closet, which was down near Joy's end of the house. On the way back, she heard the man speaking.

"Actually, ma'am, I'm the new cook."

Oh, God, not Grand-Em.

Frankie hurried up and burst through the door, ready to peel her grandmother away from the stranger. The idea of insulating him from her family was an impulse she didn't question.

"Cook?" Grand-Em looked up at him imperiously. "We have three cooks working here already. Why ever did Papa take you on?"

Grand-Em was tiny and ornate, a five-foot-two-inch waif dressed in a flowing, faded ball gown. Her long white hair, which hadn't been cut in decades, fell down her back and she had the unlined face of someone who had never been outside without a parasol. Next to Nate she looked as sturdy as a china figurine.

"Grand-Em—"

Frankie was astonished as Nate cut her off with a sharp hand. Bending at the waist, with his head properly bowed, he said, "Madam, it is my pleasure to be of service to you. My name is Nathaniel, should you need anything."

Grand-Em considered him thoughtfully and headed for the door.

"I like him," she said to no one in particular as she left.

Frankie sighed and watched her grandmother drift down the hall. The dementia that had curdled that once-active mind was a terrible thief. And to miss someone, even though you saw them daily, was an odd sort of hell.

"Who is she?" Nate asked softly.

Frankie snapped to attention, unsure how long she'd leaned against the doorjamb with the towels and sheets in her hands.

"My grandmother," she said. "Here are your linens and there are some toiletry packets in the bathroom. Washer and dryer are outside to the right, in the closet. I'm across the hall if you need anything."

As she gave the pile of whites over to him, she made the mistake of looking into his eyes. There was intrigue in them, as if he were interested in her family.

Knowing it would sound downright rude to warn him off of Grand-Em, too, Frankie kept her mouth shut as she turned away.

"I've got a question," he said.

"What?" She didn't look back at him, just stared at the pale pine floorboards as they stretched out down the hall.

"What's your name? Other than Boss, of course." The last bit wasn't mocking, more affectionate.

She'd have preferred he made fun of her.

"I'm Frankie."

"Short for Frances?"

"That's the one. Good night."

She walked across to her room and when she went to close the door, she saw he was standing in his own doorway, watching her. One arm was raised above her head with the elbow propped on the jamb. The other was balancing the linens on his hip.

He was a very sexy man, she thought, measuring his hooded eyes for an instant.

"Good night, Frances." The words were like a caress and she looked down at herself, thinking he had to be crazy. Her shirt had salad dressing spilled on it, her hair was a stringy mess by now and her pants fit her like two trash bags that had been sewn together.

She didn't reply and shut her door quickly, leaning against it and feeling her heart pound. She let her head fall back and hit the wood.

It had been so long since a man had looked at her as something other than a repository for complaints, a source of money for work he'd done or as someone who'd do his thinking for him. When was the last time she'd felt like a real woman instead of a shell that held in boiling anxiety and not much else?

David, she thought with a shock. She had to go all the way back to David.

Frankie tilted her body around until her cheek laid against the door panel.

How had time passed so fast? Day to day, dealing with the fight to keep White Caps alive, she'd been unaware that nearly a decade of her life had been eaten up.

For some stupid reason she felt like crying again, so she forced herself to cross the shallow length of her bedroom, undressing as she went. She was exhausted but she needed a shower. Throwing on a thick robe, she poked her head out into the hall.

The coast seemed clear. Nate's door was shut and she didn't hear any running water. Hightailing it to the bathroom, she jumped under the hot water, shampooed her hair, soaped herself down and was drying off in under six minutes.

As she scooted back to her room, she could have done without the stress of having to share a bathroom with the new cook. But it was sure as hell a lot better than having those hazel eyes devouring her sister.

Chapter Three

Nate woke up, feeling like someone was tickling the side of his neck. He brushed his hand over the spot a few times and then cursed the irritation.

Cracking open one eye, he wasn't particularly surprised by the fact that he didn't recognize the room he'd slept in. He wasn't sure whether he was in New York or New Mexico or what he'd agreed to do to earn the bed under him, either.

He sat up, yawned and stretched his arms out until his shoulder cracked and began to loosen up. It wasn't a bad room. Simple pine dresser, two small windows, squat ceiling. Its main selling points were that it was clean and quiet. Bed was fully functional. He'd slept like a baby.

Nate leaned forward, looking out of a window. In the distance, through a hedge, he could see a lake.

And everything came back as he pictured a woman with brunette hair and heavy framed glasses.

Frankie.

He laughed softly and tried to push off whatever was still on his neck.

Man, that was one frustrating woman but damn, he liked her. That lockjaw tenacity and take-no-prisoners, my-way-or-the-highway attitude piqued his interest something crazy. All that strength and defiance made him want to get under her hard-driving exterior. Go behind those glasses. Take off those baggy clothes of hers and let her unleash her aggression all over his body.

He shook his head, remembering the vehemence with which she'd warned him off Angel. There was no need to worry there. If he'd seemed taken by the girl when he'd first walked in the kitchen, it was because her fragile beauty was unusual, not because he was attracted to it. In fact, the strawberry blonde made him think about food, not sex. He wanted to sit her down and feed her pasta until she put on a few pounds.

No, Angel wasn't for him. He liked women, not girlie girls, and Frankie's kind of strength, even if it could get annoying, was a virtue he couldn't get enough of.

He wondered what it would take to loosen her up so he had a chance with her. She didn't strike him as the drinking kind, somehow. Much too self-controlled. And she probably wasn't into jewelry because she didn't wear any of it. Flowers? Having faced off her level stare, tender blooms seemed frivolous.

Maybe she wouldn't mind a good, hard kiss or two.

Nate let out his breath in a whistle as he imagined the possibilities and swung his legs over the side. Putting his feet on the cool floor, he scratched the side of his neck and the delirious relief instantly made him suspicious. He stood up, felt his ankle check in with a shot of pain, and limped over to the mirror. As he leaned in, he cursed. Running from his left ear down to above his collarbone, there were three rows of tiny blisters, a little plow field of misery.

Poison ivy.

Those leafy greens cushioning his fall had seemed innocent enough, but he should have known better. In the Adirondacks, the stuff grew like a carpet at the sides of roads and trails. He was lucky that most of him had been covered by the jacket and none of the leaves had connected with his face, but it was still going to be a pain in the ass to deal with.

He grabbed a towel and hit the bathroom. Frankie had mentioned there were two parties staying overnight, so he figured he better hustle downstairs to make breakfast. Ten minutes later, wearing the same clothes he'd had on the day before and with his hair damp, he headed for the kitchen.

The first thing he did was crack open the walk-in refrigerator and take inventory. There wasn't much. Eggs and milk, generic cheeses like cheddar and Monterey Jack. Some fresh veggies of the diner variety like iceberg lettuce, cucumbers, and carrots. As he was heading out, he saw a lone box of fresh blueberries.

At least breakfast would be covered, he thought, grabbing the carton.

As for the rest of the meals, he was in trouble. If he were cooking for a bunch of five-year-olds, he was good to go because he could whip up a fleet of grilled cheese sandwiches. But those guests snoozing away in the front bedrooms were not going to be satisfied with kiddy chow. He was going to have to order some supplies, nothing flashy, but enough to make some real food. He needed feta and goat cheese, some cilantro and scallions, heads of cauliflower and cabbage. Artichokes.

He went next door to the meat locker, figuring he'd find a graveyard. Instead, there was a good-looking side of beef, a hefty leg of lamb, and a turkey. That all gave him hope.

Nate resisted scratching the side of his neck and took the cardboard box over to the stove. It was close to 6:00 a.m. so there was plenty of time to make some killer blueberry muffins. A half hour later, he'd just taken the first batch out of the oven when he heard footsteps. Frankie's sister appeared at the bottom of the stairs.

He smiled. "Well, good morning there, Angel."

"Those look wonderful," she said, coming over to the muffins. She leaned down and breathed deeply.

"You should try one."

Joy shook her head. "They're for the guests."

"This is only the first batch. And you look like you could use breakfast." His eyes flickered over the bathrobe that hung off her like a tent.

She brought the lapels closer together and crossed her arms over her chest, as if trying to conjure bulk out of the terry cloth.

"Is there some way I can help you?" she asked, as if to distract him.

"You can make the coffee. Were the tables set last night?"

"No. But I can do that, too."

"Great." Nate frowned, moving his head around and wincing. That itching was going to drive him nuts.

"Are you okay?"

"For a guy whose neck is on fire, I'm fine." He pointed to the left side. "Poison ivy."

"Oh, that's terrible." Joy came in for a closer look.

"Can't say I'm crazy for it myself."

Frankie stretched, feeling unusually well-rested, and glanced at the clock.

"Aw, damn it!"

She'd forgotten to set the alarm the night before and it was now nearly a quarter of seven. Moving fast, she leaped out of bed and changed into a fresh white shirt and a clean pair of her standard black pants. She needed to get prepped for breakfast, the tables hadn't been set and there was a vegetable delivery due soon that would have to be accepted and inventoried.

She was pulling back her hair and twisting it into a ball when she froze. There was a delicious smell in the air, something that seemed to suggest muffins or scones.

Nate must be up already.

Frankie moved even faster.

She flew down the stairs and was running into the kitchen when she stopped dead in her tracks.

In the shallow space between the stove and the island, the cook and her sister were standing close enough to be kissing, his head bent down low, Joy balancing up on her tiptoes as if she were whispering something in his ear. Was her sister touching him? On the neck? Wearing nothing but a bathrobe?

"Sorry to interrupt," Frankie said loudly. "But maybe we should be thinking about breakfast?"

Joy stepped away from the man with a blush, while Nate looked over calmly.

"Breakfast is ready," he said, pointing to a tray of beautiful muffins. "The guests aren't up yet."

"Joy? Would you mind giving me and Mr.—" she paused, not even knowing his last name "—ah—him a minute alone?"

Her sister left the room as Frankie glared at Nate. "What part of stay away don't you understand?"

He turned and opened the oven, inspecting what was inside. "You always this cheerful in the morning?"

"Answer me."

"How'd you like some coffee?"

"Damn it, you want to tell me what you were doing with my sister?"

"Not particularly."

The more forceful she came at him, the calmer he seemed to get and irritation fanned the brushfire in her chest. "I thought we had an agreement. You stay away from her or you get out."

He laughed and shook his head while reaching for some side towels. He began folding them up into thick squares. "Just what do you think I was going to do? Take her down on this floor, rip open that robe of hers and—"

Frankie squeezed her eyes shut and cut him off. "There's no reason to be crude."

"No reason for you to be worried, either."

She looked at him, thinking she wasn't about to fall for the denial. When it came to women, a man who looked like him was probably about as trustworthy as a thief facing an open door. And, if he was capable of melting even her with those hazel eyes, Joy wouldn't stand a chance.

God, what had she brought into their house? And she hadn't checked his references… What if he was a convicted felon? A serial rapist?

Frankie began to imagine all sorts of terrible, *America's Most Wanted* scenarios with her sister as the victim. If anything ever happened to Joy, Frankie would never forgive herself—

"Poison ivy," he said dryly.

She forced herself to halt the spiral of paranoia. "What?"

"She was looking at my poison ivy. See?" He pointed to the side of his neck and she squinted at him. "You can come closer, I don't bite. Unless I'm asked to."

In spite of his half smile, Frankie sidled up to him and leaned in. Sure enough, there were the telltale streaks of blisters running up his skin to just under his hairline.

"That must itch terribly," she said, by way of offering an apology.

"Yeah, it's no fun." He turned back to the stove and took out another tin of the most gorgeous, golden-topped muffins she'd ever seen. The smell was something north of heaven.

"You want one?" he asked. "I tried to get your sister to have a go at them but she shut me down."

He took a muffin out and pulled it apart even though it steamed with heat. Spreading butter on the inside, which quickly melted and glistened, he offered her half.

She paused and then took the piping hot piece. Unlike him, she had to shuffle it around in her hands, and when she put some in her mouth, she had to cool it off by breathing over it.

She chewed a little and then closed her eyes so she could savor the taste.

He laughed with satisfaction. "Not bad, huh?"

He was one hell of cook, she thought. But she was still going to check his references.

"They're—ah, wonderful." She paused. "Listen, I'll need the name and number of your most recent employer. And your last name. I forgot to ask last night."

"Walker. Last name is Walker."

Frankie frowned, thinking she'd heard of the name somewhere. And no, not on Court TV.

Before she could ask about it, he said, "And the last joint I worked at was down in New York. La Nuit. Ask for Henri. He'll give it to you straight."

Frankie widened her eyes. Now, La Nuit she'd definitely heard of. It was one of those four-star restaurants that got featured in the glossy magazines the guests left behind in their rooms. How had someone like him come to work in a place like that?

"Now, about supplies," he said. "When do deliveries come?"

"Saturday and Wednesday noontime for veggies and meats. Dairy comes Mondays. Fridays also, if we need them to."

They hadn't for the past year.

"Great. What's the number? Maybe I can catch the produce guy."

"You want to talk with Stu?"

Nate frowned. "Yeah. Unless he's a mind reader."

"I do the ordering. Tell me what you want."

"I won't know that until I have a sense of what I can get."

She gestured sharply over to the walk-ins. "You can get what's already in there."

There was a pause and then he crossed his arms over his sizable chest. "I thought you wanted me to be the cook."

Facing off at him, Frankie found there was plenty of

steel behind his laid-back facade—which made it seem a little more plausible that he could have worked in a place like La Nuit. "I do."

"So let me take care of business."

She was tempted to ask just whose kitchen he thought he was standing in, but took a deep breath instead.

"As you've so graciously pointed out, White Caps isn't exactly thriving. I have to make sure we stick to the budget and that means I don't want some guy in the kitchen throwing money out the door indiscriminately."

Nate pointed to the dining room. "You want to put asses in those chairs? You want those guests to come back? Then you need to set good food on those tables, not serve stuff fit for a nursery school. You've got to spend money to make money, sweetheart."

She laughed and eyed his well-worn clothes. "What would you know about money? Or running a restaurant, for that matter?"

He leaned in close and she stopped smiling. "You might want to dial down the attitude, considering you don't know much about me. Other than the fact that you really need me over your stove."

She could feel her eyes widen of their own accord. It was a new experience to have someone stand up to her and she took a step back as she collected herself.

"All I need to know is that you work for me. Which means you do what I say."

He stared at her long and hard and she thought for a moment he was going to walk out. She had a flash of anxiety as she thought about last night's chicken fiasco and what would have happened if he hadn't shown up when he did. Still, she knew if he couldn't take orders she didn't want him in the kitchen. His theory about spending money was probably sound in a lot of situations but not when she had less than five thousand dollars in the checking account. Running a business that was teetering on the edge was a balancing act and that meant she had to know where every penny was. He could no doubt blow the whole wad on fancy stuff that would only go to waste, leaving them with nothing to cover the food costs of the following week.

Or the plumber who was coming in an hour.

Frankie blew out her breath and noted his hand was creeping up his neck as he stared at her. "Look, why don't you pull together a wish list and I'll see what I can do, okay? And don't scratch that neck. When I go to town this morning, I'll get you some calamine lotion."

Frankie turned away, thinking she had no more time to waste arguing. She had to try and locate some invoices in her damp office. And figure out where she was going to find the money for the plumber.

Chapter Four

Nate braced his arms against the stainless steel counter and bit back the curse teasing his tongue.

What did she think he was going to do, order truffles, *foie gras* and blowfish? He knew damn well they were on a shoestring and he had no interest in bringing the place down. He understood the kind of pressure she was under and he was here to help, not make things more difficult.

But he needed some real supplies.

He thought about it and decided to humor her for a little while. Make lists for her to review. Prove he could be trusted. And when she realized he had half a brain, she'd back off. As general manager, she should be marketing the place, following up with customers for feedback, balancing the books. She did not need to concern herself with whether he ordered five or six heads of romaine.

God, when was the last time he'd submitted an order list for review?

After a quick look around the kitchen for some paper, he headed for her office. As he walked in, he found her gripping the edge of her desk and throwing her whole body into the thing. In spite of all the effort, it wasn't moving from underneath the gaping, dripping hole in the ceiling.

"Let me help," he said.

Her head jerked toward him. "I'll be fine."

She wasn't going to be fine. The desk was made of mahogany and weighed about as much as a small car.

Ignoring her, he walked over and picked up one corner. Pulling the thing out from under the exposed pipes, he put it to rest under a window that had a lake view. Then he grabbed the heavy chair and carried it across the room.

"Do you have any paper?" he asked when he was finished.

"Er—in the closet."

She seemed flustered by his initiative so he took what he needed and left her alone, thinking that woman was going to have to start relying on him.

Frankie hung up the phone and stared at it. After a glowing report from the owner of La Nuit, it appeared as if she'd won the lottery when Nate walked through her back door.

A graduate of the Culinary Institute of America. A classically trained chef who had worked in Paris. Who'd have thought? Assuming that Henri guy was on the up-and-up, and her instincts told her he was, Nate was a gift from God.

Which got her thinking…if he stayed long enough, maybe he could help put them back on the map. At least with the locals. And then they could—

Frankie looked up and saw Nate standing in her doorway.

Trying to hide her surprise, she lifted her eyebrows and waited for him to speak.

"Here's my list, Boss." His voice was relaxed, the term almost an endearment.

He came forward and dropped the sheet of lined paper on the desk. His handwriting was all in capitals and very neat. The list itself was ordered logically by food group, also including his meat and dairy requirements.

"I assumed we wouldn't have more than ten people a night for the next seven days so I've kept it light. And just so you know, I'm going to redo your menu. It's old and boring."

She nodded and looked up, narrowing her stare. "I spoke with Henri just now."

Nate smiled. "How is the old buzzard?"

"He told me you were…very good."

"Precisely why I gave you his name. Figured if you heard it from him you wouldn't worry about me so much. And by the way, I don't have a criminal record and the only time I was in a police car was when I was in college and went skinny-dipping in the Charles River by mistake. My father had a lot to say about that one but I wasn't formally charged. Oh—but I do have about thirty outstanding parking tickets in New York City."

Frankie frowned in an attempt to keep a smile off her face. "Let me ask you something."

"Shoot."

"Why would someone with your background and training want to work here?"

He shrugged. "I need the money. And it's just for the summer."

"But why don't you find somewhere like La Nuit to work? Down in the city. You could be making a lot more."

Frankie closed her mouth, thinking she should shut up. Was she actually trying to talk him into going somewhere else? Because he was right—she did need him.

Nate considered her for a long moment, as if debating how up-front to be. "A buddy and I are going to buy our own restaurant. We've been looking for the last four months in New York, Boston, D.C. and Montreal, but the right opportunity hasn't come along." He grinned. "Or maybe it's more like we haven't found a place we can afford yet. I've been living off my savings and we need that money for a down payment to secure a small business loan. Right about the time my car broke down, I'd decided to find summer work and then resume the hunt in the fall. Your place is as good as any."

Frankie looked down, absurdly hurt. To her, White Caps wasn't just any place. It was home, it was family, it was…everything. But to a stranger, of course, it would just be a bunch of walls and a roof.

"I guess that makes sense."

"Besides, how can I resist the opportunity to work for someone like you?"

She glanced up. "Like me?"

His gaze drifted from her eyes to her lips. Her breath stopped.

He was looking at her as if he wanted to kiss her, she thought. He truly was.

Time slowed, then halted altogether. She looked away from him, unable to stand the tension.

"Hey, sweetheart," he said softly.

She braced herself and met his eyes again, thinking that the casual endearment really shouldn't please her.

"Smile for me and don't hide it this time."

She flushed. "Maybe later."

Nate's lips lifted slightly, as if he enjoyed her show of spirit. "I'm willing to wait."

And then he went back out to the kitchen.

Frankie put her head in her hands, propping the weight up by her elbows. She was not the kind of woman who fell for romance. She really wasn't. But, in a matter of moments, he could completely disarm her with that charm of his. Somehow, even if it was a ruse, just some throwaway words to him, his husky voice had the power to short out her brain and turn on her body's boiler system.

This was not good.

In the middle of all the chaos, being attracted to her new cook—*chef*—was a complication she didn't need.

The phone rang and she picked it up with relief, ready to be distracted. It was, unfortunately, someone canceling their reservation for the following weekend. When she hung up, she looked through the window. Out on the lawn, which needed to be mowed again, there were a pair of chipmunks racing around.

An old memory drifted through her mind. She saw Joy and Alex and her much younger self in the midst of an Easter egg hunt. Joy had found only one egg, but that was because she'd been looking for the bright pink one in particular and had stopped once she got it. Alex had found three, but then lost interest and climbed up a tree to see how high he could go. Frankie had scampered around, retrieved all the other eggs and divvied them up between the baskets equally. Finding them had been easy enough to do. She'd helped her mother hide them.

That was so long ago, she thought. Back when their parents had seemed like fixed objects in the sky, a sure-fire, two-pronged orientation system to the world. That feeling of safety, however illusory, had been so powerful.

God, she missed them.

When the chipmunks got bored with playing keep-away and disappeared into the lilac hedges, she let the past go.

Measuring the lawn, and envisioning hours of pushing the ancient manual mower, she looked back down at the desk. Next to Nate's list was the letter from the bank—the one that reminded her she'd been behind on the mortgage payments for six months in a row. Her banker, Mike Roy, had written on the bottom of the form letter: *Let's talk soon—we'll work something out.*

She was lucky she had Mike to deal with. He'd been head of the local bank for almost five years and had always been fair. Maybe a little more than fair. She'd gotten behind in years past, especially at the end of the long dry spell caused by winter. The summer season provided her with the opportunity to get caught up and she'd always managed to get things under control again. At least until last summer. For the first time, she'd gone into the winter still behind, which meant she had an even bigger hole to dig out of this season.

She worried that selling the place might be inevitable. She'd been rejecting the idea out of hand for years, but it looked as if the unthinkable might become the unavoidable.

With a nauseous swell, Frankie imagined packing up her family's home. Her family's heritage. She pictured herself transferring the title to the house and the land to someone else. Walking away, forever.

No.

The protest didn't come from her head. It came from her heart. And the strength of it flooded through her body, making her hands shake.

There had to be a way to make it work. There just had to be. She refused to sell the only thing left of her parents, of her family. She had worked hard all of her adult life to keep White Caps. She wasn't going to stop now just because the stakes seemed more stacked than ever against her.

She thought of Nate. A fine French chef. Maybe he could, as he put it, get some asses back in those chairs. And she could run some specials on the Lincoln room in the newspapers around the area. There was always Labor Day to look forward to. They already had three rooms booked and usually they had a full house. And hadn't she read in the paper the other day that tourism was on the upswing after a couple of hard years?

The tide was going to turn in their favor and it would be a damn shame to quit just before things got better. She only had to have a little faith.

Frankie checked her watch and picked up her purse. She needed to go into town to make a deposit before the bank closed at noon and there were a few odds and ends she had to pick up. As soon as she got back, she was going to take care of the lawn. It always seemed as if the moment she finished pushing that arthritic mower around, she had to start on the acres of grass all over again. She'd asked George to do it once but it had looked like a shag carpet when he was finished. It was easier to do the job by herself than try and talk him through the process a second time.

She passed through the kitchen, where Nate was working over the stove, and called upstairs. "Joy, I'm heading into town, you need anything?"

"Can Grand-Em and I come?"

Frankie was tempted to say no. She wanted to get back before the vegetable delivery came and going anywhere with their grandmother was a production.

Joy appeared at the top of the stairs. "Please?"

"Okay, but hurry." Frankie wondered what the big deal was as she glanced over at Nate. "That smells good. What are you making?"

"Stock. I'm putting what's left of that chicken to good use." He turned back to a cutting board and started in on an onion. Half of the thing was reduced to a pile of perfectly cut little squares in moments. The other half he cut in long shreds. "Hey, I told the tow truck I called to move Lucille here, okay? I've got to figure out what's wrong with her."

And he fixes cars, she thought. As well as names them.

"Fine with me. You can put her in the barn out back."

"Thanks." He picked up the fluffy white mélange, threw it in the pot and stirred.

When Joy came downstairs with their grandmother, Frankie got a load of Grand-Em's outfit for the day. It was a lavender satin gown, and though the thing must have been fifty years old, it still looked beautiful. Somehow, Joy managed to keep all the old gowns in good shape, spending hours with a needle patching and stitching them back together, year after year. God only knew where she got the patience.

"You need anything?" Frankie asked Nate.

He looked up and grinned. "Nothing you can buy me."

With a wink thrown to Joy, he went back to his work.

As they left, Frankie's mouth was set. She wasn't sure what she resented more, his harmless flirtation or her reaction to it.

They headed out into the sunshine to her old maroon Honda. Grand-Em, who was used to being chauffeured, was eased in the back seat and Joy sat beside her. During the drive along Lake Road, the old woman narrated landmarks, commenting on the houses she'd gone to parties in years ago. It was the same patter every time, the same names, the same dates. The speech seemed to have a calming effect on her, as if the old familiarity pulled her mind together temporarily, and Joy responded at the right intervals while Frankie drove.

Downtown, such as it was, was built around a square of lawn that had four thick-trunked maples at each of the corners. In the center, there was a six-sided white gazebo that was a point of pride to residents. Big enough to house the twenty-piece orchestra that played there twice a summer, it was mostly used by tourists as a backdrop for pictures. Glowing in the morning sun, it stood out against the green lawn like a silvery cage.

The Lake Road split in two around the gazebo, rejoining on the far side. Fronting the streets, were the local bank, Adirondack Trust & Savings, a drugstore known as Pills, the post office and Mickey's Groceries. There were also some touristy shops that sold Adirondack-style trinkets, as well as a few antique stores that hiked their prices up by a factor of ten in the months between May and September. Barclay's Liquors and the Hair Stoppe were on the far end.

"I'm going into the bank and the post office," Frankie said, parallel parking into an open space. "Why don't you two wait here?"

"Sure," Joy murmured while craning her neck around and looking at the cars parked on either side of the road. With all the Independence weekend visitors, they were a fancier lot than the local traffic. The Jaguars, Mercedes and Audis signified that the owners of the mansions were back in residence.

As Frankie got out, she wondered who her sister was searching for.

He would be up this weekend, Joy thought. He always came for the Fourth of July.

Grayson Bennett drove a black BMW 645Ci. Or at least that had been what he'd come in last year. Two years ago, he'd had a big, dark red Mercedes. Before that, it had been a Porsche. His first car had been an Alfa Romeo convertible.

For a woman who didn't care about the automotive industry in the slightest, Joy knew a hell of a lot about cars, thanks to him.

There were a few people walking the clean, pale sidewalks and she sifted through them. Gray was easy to pick out of the crowd. He was tall, imposing and he didn't walk places, he marched. He also tended to wear sunglasses, dark ones that played off his black hair and made him look even more intense.

She realized that Gray would be thirty-six this year. His birthday bash, held every year at the Bennett estate, was one of the highlights of the social season although it wasn't as if she or Frankie were invited. The Moorehouses had once mixed with the Bennetts regularly, back in Grand-Em's day, but with the declining fortunes of Joy's family, the two had ceased moving in the same circles.

That didn't mean she couldn't picture a different scenario, however.

A favorite daydream of hers was to imagine going to that party, dressed beautifully, floating among his guests until he noticed her and saw her as she really was. As a woman, not some child. He would take her into his arms and kiss her and then they would go off somewhere quiet together.

In real life, their encounters were a lot less romantic. In the summer months, if she saw him around town, she'd plant herself in his path. He would stop and she'd hold her breath, willing him to remember her name. He always did. He'd smile down at her and sometimes even take off his sunglasses as he asked about her family.

From the left, she saw a BMW approach and she leaned forward. It was the wrong kind.

As she settled back against the seat, letting Grand-Em natter on about the opening of the town library back in 1936, she couldn't ignore how one-sided her attraction was.

She looked down at her bare ring finger. If she kept up the teenage fantasy, she knew she was on the winding trail to spinsterhood. She'd probably end up weird Auntie Joy who'd never married and smelled like mothballs and denatured perfume.

Now there was a picture.

If they could only leave White Caps and move somewhere with more people her own age, she might be able to get Gray Bennett off her mind. Maybe it wasn't his fantastic good looks or his dark, sexy voice or those pale blue eyes.

Maybe it was just a lack of viable alternatives.

"Did you know that my fourth great-grandfather built that gazebo?" Grand-Em inquired. She wasn't looking for an answer. It was an invitation for a prompting.

"Really. Tell me about it," Joy murmured, putting her hand down in her lap.

"It was in 1849. There had been a terrible winter that year and the old one had collapsed because of the snow. Great Grand Pa-Pa declared the structure unsafe…."

Grand-Em spoke with a proper intonation, her words carefully considered as if they were a gift to the listener and therefore must be chosen with respect and affection. And Joy usually found them fascinating. She loved listening to the old stories, particularly about the balls and the clothes.

But not today.

After nearly a decade of pining for a man she couldn't have, Joy was struck with how pathetic her attraction to Gray was. Pinning hopeless dreams on a fantasy was like feeding yourself with chocolate. A great short-term buzz with no lasting value.

It really was time to give up. The focus on Gray had gotten her nowhere except to the edge of obsession. And the fantasy, like her, was getting old.

Joy stared out at the crowd. Where was he—

"I beg your pardon," Grand-Em remarked. "But the gazebo is out the other window. Whatever are you looking for?"

"The man I want to marry," Joy muttered, turning her head so Grand-Em would continue. "As crazy as that sounds."

"You are engaged?"

Joy shook her head, thinking that was never going to happen. "Please continue, Grand-Em. You were saying about the gazebo?"

Grand-Em nodded and started to talk again.

Moments later, Frankie jogged up to the car. She put the mail on the passenger seat in front and tossed over a little white paper bag that read Thomas Pills Rx.

"We're doing the gazebo story now?" she said, starting the car.

Joy nodded and thought maybe she'd ask Frankie for some advice. She sure could use some perspective.

Frankie threw the car in gear, did an illegal U-turn and bolted for home. "Listen, if you can handle lunch service, I'm going to do the lawn and water the window boxes. We had a cancellation for next weekend which means we'll only have one couple. One. Can you believe it? God, we used to be packed."

Or maybe she'd just keep to herself, Joy thought.

"Oh, hey, you'll never believe who I ran into."

Grand-Em coughed loudly, aware that another conversation was interrupting her story. Frankie ignored the signal, so Joy turned and patted her grandmother's hand. The last thing they needed was for her to get hyper, which was what could happen when her narratives were cut off.

"It's okay," Joy said gently. "Keep going."

Grand-Em smiled and started to talk again.

"Gray Bennett," Frankie said.

Joy flipped her head around. "What did you say?"

"Gray Bennett. I saw him in the post office. He's up for the weekend and said he was thinking about staying all summer."

Joy's heart started kicking in her chest. "Really? The whole summer?"

Grand-Em coughed again.

"Yeah." Frankie darted out around a car and splashed back into the right lane as they went up Yellow-belly Hill.

Joy stared out the window, trying to tamp down on her excitement and losing the battle. "Er—how did he look?"

"Oh, you know, Gray. He always looks good."

Yes, she knew that. All too well. But she wanted to know everything. How long his hair was, was he wearing shorts, did he look happy?

God, did he have a ring on his finger?

She grimaced, thinking she would surely have read about it if he'd gotten married. The wedding of someone like him would make it into the papers.

"He asked about you, by the way."

Joy froze. "Really?"

Frankie nodded and then started saying something about the plumber.

As Joy looked out of the window, the sounds of her sister and her grandmother talking at the same time filled the inside of the car. Trapping her.

But when she began to think about Gray, she started to smile.

Chapter Five

Frankie wiped her arm across her forehead, bent forward at a steeper angle and pushed the mower harder. The blades whirled and grass was kicked up in a green flurry until it covered her running shoes. If she went fast enough, she could probably finish the side- and lake-facing portions of the three-acre lawn by the afternoon.

"Frankie!"

She lifted her head and saw Joy in a window.

"Phone! It's Mike Roy."

Frankie stopped pushing as her mind jumped to conclusions. Why was her banker calling her in the middle of a holiday weekend?

"Frankie?"

"Coming."

Leaving the mower where it was, she was heading

for the back door when Stu pulled up with his truck full of vegetables.

"I'll be with you in a minute," she called out.

He nodded, lit up a cigarette and seemed perfectly happy to wait.

As she steamed through the kitchen, Nate looked up from the stove. "The vegetables here?"

She nodded. "I'll be out in a—"

"Great," he said, heading for the door.

Frankie paused, wanting to reel him back in. As a homeowner indebted up to her eyeballs, however, her banker took precedence.

In her office, she straightened her clothes before picking up the receiver, telling herself Mike Roy wouldn't be able to hear the fact that she was sweaty and disheveled. She grabbed the phone and imagined him telling her he was foreclosing on the mortgage. And selling White Caps to a real estate developer who was going to run two hundred condos with hot tubs up the mountain.

"Hi, Mike," she said. "What's up?"

Have you turned into a shark after five years of being a lamb?

"I was wondering if I can bring someone by to visit White Caps. He's in town over the weekend and I'm showing him around. I can't very well leave out the place where Lincoln slept."

She let out her breath with relief. "Of course, bring him over anytime. We have a guest in Abe's room but I'll ask whether he'd mind if you put your head in."

"Great."

There was a pause. Her stomach clenched. "Listen, Mike, about the mortgage payments. I'd like to come in and show you my plan for covering what I owe."

"That'd be great. We'll meet next week in my office. But I'll see you in an hour or so, Frankie."

As she hung up the phone, she played the conversation over and over again, searching for clues in the man's intonation and diction. But it was like reading tea leaves, she supposed. Useless and agitating.

Across the room, she saw the simple black picture frame that held the photo of her family. It was still laying facedown after Nate had picked it off the shelf. She went over and righted it, her thumb brushing over the image of her father.

Joy put her head through the door. "Frankie? Stu needs a check."

She blinked.

"Are you okay?" Joy started across the office but Frankie went back to her desk.

"Yes, fine. Tell Stu I'll help him unload."

"Oh, that's done." Frankie frowned while Joy nodded over her shoulder. "Nate took care of it."

Frankie grabbed the checkbook and one of the inventory receipt forms she'd created and went into the kitchen.

Stu and Nate were leaning back against the kitchen counter, both with their arms crossed in front of their chests. Their heads were facing out into the room, which made sense because Stu generally preferred not to make eye contact. Nate was nodding. They were chewing the cud, she realized.

This was a surprise because Stu didn't curry well to strangers and he never seemed to say more than two words at a time.

"Hi, Stu," she said. "How much do we owe you?"

Stu took off his John Deere hat and looked at it. "Think a hundred'll cover it."

She wrote out the check, gave him the following week's order and thanked him.

"Good talking to you," Nate said.

"Yup." Stu lifted his hand as he left.

"Nice old coot," Nate remarked as the screen door slapped shut.

Bracing herself, she went into the walk-in, unsure whether she'd find a disorganized jungle or not. Fortunately, Nate's organizational skills were as good as his penmanship. The lettuce was in one corner, standing up on a plastic tray. The heads of broccoli, cauliflower and cabbage were on another shelf in milk crates. Root vegetables on the floor in a bin. Pretty much where she would have put everything.

She started making notations on her clipboard when Nate's voice came from behind her shoulder.

"Checking my work?" he said dryly as he reached over her shoulder for some celery.

Stepping out of the way of his arm, she tugged at the collar of her shirt and tightened her lips. The walk-in suddenly felt like a sauna, which meant either the compressor had finally died or she was having a hot flash.

She hid a grin. At least she could call a HVAC guy if there was a mechanical problem with the refrigerator. If her libido was acting up, she might be in trouble. She doubted there was an estrogen repairman in the Yellow Pages.

"What's all this?" he asked, coming close again.

She looked down at what she'd been writing, determined not to fixate on how his biceps were straining his T-shirt's short sleeves.

"An inventory system I developed." When he didn't leave, she tipped the paper his way and stepped back.

"It's a really helpful method of determining our food costs and measuring our prices."

She was surprised when he took the clipboard and thumbed through the pages with interest. "This is good."

"I enter everything in the computer and can pull up Excel spreadsheets of our inventory consumption, staff costs, debt financing, income. Anything that comes in or goes out the door, I have by month. Year. I can project trends, track performance." Aware she was babbling, she reached for her work and he let her take it.

"Where did you go to B-school?"

"I didn't."

His eyebrows rose. "You came up with this all by yourself?"

"I just figured out what I needed to know to make the right decisions. I wish the trends were better, of course. But I feel more in control if I know what's going on."

He looked at her, studying her thoughtfully.

"Did you need something else from the walk-in?" she asked.

His smile was lazy.

"Not right now." He nodded at the clipboard. "That's really good work."

She looked down again, trying to convince herself that the respect in his voice didn't matter to her at all. But as she started counting the broccoli again, she began to smile.

"Hey, Frankie?"

She glanced up.

"What do you have around here for a nightlife?"

It was an unexpected question and kicked up an

image of him on the prowl for women. He'd probably go for the kind who wore short skirts and belly shirts and could lay a man out flat with a pyrotechnic smile. Which meant she lost on all accounts. The only expression she had that could get a man's attention was the one she made when she was angry. And as for her wardrobe, the closest she had to anything tight was an old pair of stockings.

She pushed aside an odd disappointment. It was none of her damn business what his type was. And there was nothing wrong with loose clothes, either. She didn't like things that chaffed or had to be removed with a crowbar. And thongs were nothing more than wedgies you had to pay for the privilege of getting. Which was nuts.

Nate cocked an eyebrow, waiting for her answer.

She shrugged. "We've only got fireflies and shooting stars here at White Caps, but there is a bar in town. Somehow, though, I imagine you'd prefer something more exciting than what the Stop, Drop and Roll offers."

"That's the name of the bar?"

"It's owned by a volunteer fireman."

He smiled. "Well, I think what you have here will do just fine."

She shot him a skeptical look, refusing to read into his words. "Coming from New York City, I'm sure you'll want something with more of an edge."

"That depends on who I'm with. Sometimes quiet is better." His eyes moved down to her lips and his grin disappeared. "Sometimes, two people only need the night."

A moment later he turned away, leaving her staring after him.

Her fingers went to her mouth and she wondered whether you could be kissed without actually being kissed.

After he'd looked at her like that, she'd have to say yes.

Frankie leaned forward and put her forehead against a shelf. Oh, God, what was she getting herself into? And why now? After years of being as close to a nun as a woman could get while not actually wearing the habit and crepe-soled shoes, *now* she decides to get all hot and bothered about a man? A man who, by the way, was just passing through and would be gone by the end of the summer? Who was her employee?

She'd been busy worrying about what would happen if he got his hands on Joy, but maybe she'd do better looking into a mirror. She should probably be giving *herself* a stiff lecture about not ending up heartbroken in September. Because that was the way it would end between them. He would go back to the city. She would stay behind.

Just as it had been with David.

The cold metal pressing into her eyebrows reminded her she was standing in a walk-in. As if the pounds of vegetables and the hearty draft wouldn't have clued her in.

Frankie straightened up and looked at her inventory sheet. The orderly rows of columns were a comfort, but when she tried to get back to work, her fingers had pretty much frozen stiff and her handwriting was like a child's. She rushed through the inventory thinking that, with Nate gone, she could feel the cold through her clothes.

When she rushed out, blowing into her hands, she thought that at least the walk-in's compressor was still going strong.

* * *

Nate was happy to see the tow company's truck pull up. After greeting the guy, he walked over to the barn behind the mansion and opened the double doors, motioning the flatbed back. He knew Lucille would feel right at home. The stalls on both sides were full of dust-covered, broken-down equipment, including a riding mower, a rototiller and a snowblower.

Though maybe she'd just be depressed by the company.

When Lucille was in the barn, he paid the guy and popped her hood. After giving her engine the once-over again, he crawled beneath her and looked at her under-carriage. She'd leaked out all her oil and that was what worried him. All her hoses were plugged in and her oil pan was solid because he'd replaced it a year ago. He had a feeling her engine block might have cracked. Not encouraging.

Nate shrugged out from under the car and stood up, looking for something to clean the grime off his hands. There was nothing around so he used the edge of his T-shirt, figuring it needed to go into the wash anyway. He opened the trunk, took out his duffel bag full of clothes and was slinging the thing over his shoulder when the back door to the house slapped shut. Frankie walked out into the pale sunshine.

She was wearing a pair of shorts that gave him a clear look at her legs and they were terrific. Long, muscled from physical labor, with smooth skin. He wondered why she hid them under those god-awful black pants.

Hell, maybe it was so guys like him wouldn't hit on her. Which was what he'd been working up to when they'd been alone with all that produce.

It would explain her glasses, too.

Staying in the shadow of the barn, he watched her go over to a push mower and hike up her sleeves. She confronted the piece of equipment like she was taking on an animal she was hell-bent on training, and her mouth was moving, as if she were talking to the thing. He was more than willing to bet, if the mower hadn't been an inanimate object, it would have snapped to attention and done just as she'd asked.

Nate shook his head and leaned back against the doorjamb. He'd been on the verge of kissing her in that walk-in. The only thing that had stopped him was the danger that George or Joy could have barged in at any moment. And a deep freeze wasn't exactly the best place to make love.

Not for a couple's first time, at any rate.

Nate frowned, remembering a couple of employers or supervisors he'd been with in the past. Maybe hitting on Frankie wasn't such a good idea. White Caps was a small enterprise. And even if he was only staying two months, sixty days could feel like a lifetime under the wrong circumstances.

Frankie bent over the mower, adjusting the blade. As his eyes traveled from her ankles up to her thighs and over her hips, he shifted his weight impatiently and felt like cursing.

Sure it was probably better if he left her alone. But she did crazy things to his body and he was just the kind of meathead who'd give up an opportunity to be sensible in favor of having even one night alone with a woman like her.

He knew damn well he was going to end up asking her out. Kissing her. Hopefully, taking things even further. He was sure she was attracted to him. He could see it in her eyes. And he definitely wanted her. So there was absolutely no harm in two adults having some fun.

No harm, no foul. Just a little summer affair.

Nate winced and wondered why an ache had settled in his chest.

Ah, hell. He knew why. Frankie wasn't like the other women he'd fallen into bed with, he thought as he rubbed his sternum. She didn't parade around, looking for attention from men. In fact, all the signals she sent out were of the lay-off variety and he didn't think it was just him. She didn't seem to flirt with the male guests, either.

Although Mr. Little wasn't exactly tall, dark and handsome, granted.

Nate dropped his hand.

He hoped his conscience wasn't going to ruin what could be a terrific time between the sheets.

She started pushing and he frowned, measuring the size of the lawn around White Caps. He couldn't believe she was going to do the whole thing by herself, and then thought, of course she'd do it alone. He was tempted to go right over to her, but figured he'd give her a little time to wear herself out. He knew she'd wait until she was half dead before she'd accept help. And even then it would be under stinging protest.

Man, he liked her.

Nate went up to his bedroom, unpacked, threw some clothes in the wash and then headed out to the lawn. She'd made it all the way through the side lawn and was about to tackle the grass that ran down to the lakeshore.

He walked up to her. "Hey."

She stopped mowing and regarded him as coolly as someone sweating and panting could.

"You need some help?" He smiled as she shook her head. "I didn't think so. How about I phrase it like this. I like to mow lawns. I'd like to mow this one. How can you stand in the way of my dream?"

She wiped her forearm across her brow. "Shouldn't you be in the kitchen?"

"Daily prep is done. I've got everything under control in there right now." He eyed the sun, which had emerged from the clouds, and then her shirt, which had a dark V of sweat running from her neck to her breasts.

"So how about I spell you?" He leaned in. "You know, accepting help is not a sin."

Before she could answer him, the Littles came out onto the porch. Frankie's eyes fled to them as if they were a welcome relief so he looked over, too. Mr. Little was wearing a pastel polo shirt and khakis. So was his wife. They looked like dolls, perfectly dressed, perfectly coifed. They reminded him of his super-wealthy Walker relatives, a group of people he avoided at all costs.

"Guard of the entrance to the underworld in Greek mythology," the man said, tapping a pen at a crossword puzzle. "Eight letters."

"I'm not good at the *Times* puzzle," his wife said, sitting down in a chair out of the sun. She flipped open *Architectural Digest*. "You know that."

The man looked up with annoyance. "Yes, I do. I was talking to myself."

Nate refocused on Frankie. "So what do you say?"

"God!" Mr. Little exclaimed. "This is impossible. Guard of the entrance—"

Nate rolled his eyes and spoke over his shoulder. "Cerberus."

Mr. Little glanced up as if someone had lobbed a rot-ten tomato at him. He eyed Nate's ratty T-shirt, his gaze lingering on the oil stains.

"I beg your pardon?"

"Cerberus," Nate repeated. "You want me to spell it for you?"

Frankie tugged at his arm. "Excuse us, Mr. Little."

But the man wasn't listening. He'd pursed his lips and was busying counting off the letters. He looked up. "Ah—you're right."

"I know," Nate said, just as Frankie pulled him out of the man's sight. "What's the matter?"

"Do us all a favor and don't upset that guy. Once he gets rolling, he can go on forever. This morning, he was upset when a boat went by on the lake and woke him up. He wanted to know if I could post buoys out in front warning that noise pollution will not be tolerated. I thought he'd never shut up," she whispered. "He's impossible."

"Doesn't know his classical myths very well, either. Now, about the lawn."

She frowned, considered him strangely, and then shook her head as if clearing it. "Listen, I need you in the kitchen, not doing grounds work. I appreciate your offer—"

"But you'd really rather do it yourself," he finished. "You know, with the amount of work that needs to get done around this place, you should be looking for volunteers, not turning them away. You have better things to do with your time than mowing the lawn."

He cocked an eyebrow, challenging her to contradict him. Her mouth opened as if she was going to, but then she closed it slowly. She put her hands on her hips and looked down at her grass-covered sneakers.

"Don't tell me you're trying to turn over a new leaf

or something," he said, thinking it was very possible he was developing a crush on her. "I'd rather be berated by you than have to watch you trying to be good."

She laughed and then cut the sound short. "I really want to argue with you."

"Because I'm being insubordinate?" He grinned.

"Worse. Because you're probably right." She scanned the lawn, the lilac bushes, the boathouse down at the shore. As she looked around, she seemed so solitary, so self-contained. So tired.

"How long ago did you buy this place?" he asked.

"Buy?" She squinted up at him. "My sixth great-grandfather built it."

"The last stand," he murmured. No wonder she was hanging in.

"Something like that."

She turned her head to the house, running her eyes over it as if she was a mother inspecting a child for cuts and bruises. He watched as she lingered on the gutter, which was listing away from the roof edge. He was willing to bet she was making a mental note to fix it and that she'd do it herself.

The idea of Frankie high up on a ladder made him uneasy.

"So you grew up here?"

"Born, raised, the whole bit." Her eyes went to the lake.

"Where are your parents—are they retired?"

She looked away from the water abruptly. "No, they're dead."

Her tone of voice told him their conversation was going to be over in a matter of seconds so he didn't dawdle in offering his condolences.

"I'm sorry."

He watched as she shut down in front of him and the change happened so fast, it was like having a door slammed in his face. Her eyes went impassive and her expression assumed a deliberate calm that made him wonder about the emotions underneath.

"Thank you, but it was a long time ago," she said.

"You know, I lost a parent five years ago. We didn't get along, but the death changed everything, anyway." He didn't want to mention it was an improvement because clearly what had been left for her was not. "It takes quite a while to get over losing a parent, much less both of them."

She shrugged and he mined the angles of her face and the color of her eyes for some sign she would let him in.

Eventually, he said, "So about the lawn."

She nodded downward, towards his feet. "I don't know that you should be pushing a mower around with that ankle of yours."

"I'll go until I can't go anymore."

"Funny, that's my motto, too."

As she smiled and looked back out to the lake, he noticed that her glasses were smudged. Moving quickly, so she wouldn't have a chance to jerk away, he took them off her face.

"What are you doing?"

He easily stepped out of her reach while she tried to grab them. "Cleaning your glasses."

"Give them back."

He rubbed one side and then the other with the clean corner of his shirt while moving around as she tried to take them. Lifting the lenses up to the sun and high over her head, he measured his work.

"There. All better."

Intending to slip them back on the bridge of her nose, he looked down just as she leaped up. Her body collided with his and he gripped her around the waist to keep them from falling over.

As soon as she was in his arms, he felt as if he was out of control and on the way home at the same time. She must have felt it, too. Her lips parted in surprise as she looked up into his face.

Those eyes, he thought. Those miraculous blue eyes should never be hidden. At least not from him.

"Put me down," she whispered. "I'm too heavy."

But she wasn't. He felt as if he could hold her forever.

Nate leaned in, getting his lips close to her ear. "Do you really want me to?"

He felt her nod into his shoulder and told himself he could still keep her in his arms even if her feet were touching the ground. It would be easier to kiss her that way, too.

He held his breath as he let her slide slowly down his body. When she was standing on her own, her breasts were against his chest and her hips pressed into what was quickly becoming his rigid arousal. He waited for a moment, wondering if she was going to pull back. Her hands were on his shoulders, laying lightly against the material of his shirt. She seemed to be focusing somewhere to his left, but she didn't look as if she were really seeing anything.

He put a fingertip under her chin and tilted her face up. Her eyes came to his reluctantly.

"Hi," he said. Stupidly.

But what else could he say? My God, woman, where

have you been all my life? Or the ever popular, how'd you like to go upstairs, right now, and get naked with me?

A blush hit her cheeks, spread down her neck and he knew he'd ruined the moment by talking. Breaking free, she snatched the glasses back and fumbled to put them on. When she got one of the ear pieces stuck in her ear, she had to try it again.

"If you'll excuse me—"

As she turned away, he reached for her, taking her hand.

"Don't go." He wanted to tell her he wasn't some scumbag macking on her randomly. He liked her. He wanted to get to know her better. They could go slowly.

Even though it would probably kill him. Light speed seemed like a lazy jog to him at the moment.

Frankie lifted her chin and shot him a level smile. "But I wouldn't want to hold you up."

He frowned, thinking that he didn't have anything to do but stare into those eyes of hers. "From what?"

"Mowing the lawn," she said and yanked her hand free.

As she raced around the corner, he threw his head back and laughed.

Chapter Six

Hope he enjoys the afternoon, Frankie thought, as she stepped under the shower. Rinsing off her sweat, she pictured Nate slaving over that old mower, cursing the moment he'd *volunteered* for the job.

She squeezed out some shampoo and rubbed it into her hair, stirring up a lather. Her hands stilled.

God, that man. He was so…inconvenient.

Actually, there were quite a number of more accurate words she could have used but they all scared her. She didn't want to describe him, even to herself, as sexy or compelling. Or exciting. Even though he was of all those.

And to top it all off, he seemed to be attracted to her.

Which meant he was delusional, too.

When her eyes started stinging, she ducked under the spray. She rinsed, turned off the water and stepped out onto the bath mat. After toweling dry, she wiped the mirror clean with her forearm and leaned in for a closer look.

What did he see in her, she wondered, pulling a length of hair straight out from her scalp. She let go and felt it hit her shoulder with a wet slap.

As she stared at herself through the streaks on the mirror, she was not exactly inspired. Her hair was thick and long but the color was a dull brown. Her eyes were nice enough, she supposed, spaced well and lined thickly with lashes. She flashed her teeth. They were in great shape, straight and white, just as her father's had been.

Okay, so she wasn't completely gone. But she wouldn't exactly give Miss America a run for the money.

Frankie let the mirror fog up again, dried her hair and told herself to forget about the midair collision with Nate. He certainly would, the moment he went down to the Stop, Drop and Roll and got a good look at a few of the local hardies. Hell, if she had any luck, he'd head there tonight because she couldn't afford to be distracted.

But as she went to her room, she wondered *from what?* What exactly was so pressing that she didn't have ten minutes to spare in the bathroom fantasizing about some guy? It wasn't as if reliving a little thrill was dangerous. She wasn't throwing herself at him, for God's sake.

So what was the problem?

Well, for one thing, nothing that felt that good, that exciting, could possibly be harmless, she thought.

Which was why doctors told people not to overdo it in hot tubs and pregnant ladies couldn't go on roller coasters.

Besides, she wasn't a daydreamer. Fantasies, especially the romantic kind, required something she didn't have. They needed hope to flare, even if it was for a mere ten minutes in a fogged out bathroom. Thanks to David, most of her foolish optimism about love had been drilled out of her. A couple of bad dates had polished off the rest.

No, dreams were totally out of character for her. Out of context. Out of the question, really.

Just like any romance between her and her new chef.

Frankie pulled on her pants and tucked her shirt in. After brushing out her hair and twisting a scrunchie around it, she put her glasses back on and went down to the office. Sitting at the desk, she tried to balance the bank account, but she couldn't seem to get her mind focused.

On anything other than Nate.

Everything reminded her of him. Her desk because he'd moved it. The inventory sheets because he'd admired them. Her pencil…because he'd borrowed one, this morning.

God, she was desperate.

Frankie pushed her calculator away and stared across the room. Twenty-four hours ago she'd never met the man and now she couldn't get him out of her head.

But this was how it worked between the sexes, she thought. This was the biological imperative at work. David had been gone from her life for nearly ten years and she was an otherwise healthy woman. It was inevitable that someone would come along and catch her eye. Eventually.

Except the attraction was a surprise. Sure, there had been some handsome guests over the years, even some who had been single. But they hadn't been interested and neither had she. Wealthy men were a turnoff to begin with for her, because they reminded her of David, and the rich guys usually liked a different kind of woman entirely, anyway. And as for the indigenous Saranac Lake male, well, she just couldn't get all that excited over them. To begin with, she knew too much about each one, small towns being what they are.

At least Nate wasn't some privileged dandy. He was a hard worker who seemed to have a clear picture of where he wanted to go. And she didn't know a thing about him, which made him mysterious. Although why that was a virtue, she couldn't begin to guess.

Frustrated because she couldn't concentrate, she decided to go check the tables for dinner set-up. It was obvious she was going to get nothing done in her office.

She pushed open the door to the dining room and frowned. Mrs. Little was leaning on one of the tables, staring out of the window, completely absorbed by something.

"Is there anything wrong?" Frankie asked.

The woman whirled around, clasping her strand of pearls. "Er—no. Nothing. At all. Excuse me."

Which meant as soon as Mrs. Little tore out of the room, Frankie went right over to the window. She put her hands on the sill and bent down, expecting to see a woodchuck or maybe a bird of some kind. City people like the Littles probably thought chipmunks were worthy of a *National Geographic* special.

Frankie's breath left her in a rush.

Holy, Mother of…

Nate was pushing the mower, making even lines in the grass. With his shirt tucked into his back pocket.

No wonder he hadn't been bothered by her weight, she thought, looking over every inch of him.

He'd just gone by the window so she had a clear shot of his back. Muscles fanned out from his spine, filling his shoulders, wrapping around his rib cage. He was built big and hard, and when he turned and started coming towards her, she saw the front of him was as cut as the back.

It made sense, she supposed, given that muscling around a kitchen was a physically demanding job. Cooks were constantly lifting things, moving, on their feet. Still, considering how he looked, she figured there were some serious genetics at work and some weight training, too. Had to be. No one got shoulders that wide from picking pans off a stove top, even if the things were full of water.

No wonder Mrs. Little had been so entranced.

Frankie stepped out of the way before he could see her. Looking blindly around the dining room, she couldn't remember why she'd left her office.

Later that night, after the kitchen had been closed down and everyone had gone upstairs, Frankie finally got some work done. The day had been worthless. Between stewing about Nate and waiting for Mike Roy to bring his mystery guest over, she'd been distracted and jittery.

Mike had finally called at six and apologized, explaining that his friend had been delayed and wouldn't be arriving until next week. She'd been gracious because it wasn't as if she'd had another option. She couldn't very well tell him that an impending visit from him, with or without a hanger-on, was enough to make her want to make jam.

The urge to melt down piles of fruit and put the residue into little jars with wax seals was her response to stress. It was one of Frankie's few inheritances from her mother and she'd have much preferred it if the woman had been a knitter. Bags of yarn were easier to deal with, and there were the seasonal problems of trying to find fresh strawberries in upstate New York if Frankie hit a rough spot in the winter.

Then again, you couldn't put an Irish sweater on toast, so the compulsion wasn't a complete loss.

Frankie took off her glasses and rubbed her eyes. It was almost midnight. Unless she was planning to sleep at her desk, she'd better make a run for the stairs. Judging from her bobbing head, she had another ten minutes until she'd be sound asleep, wherever she was.

As she slowly climbed the back stairs, she thought of Nate and wondered what he wore to bed. Boxers? Briefs? The preoccupation with his night-time wardrobe didn't shame her in the slightest. Considering the depths to which she'd sunk while picturing herself kissing him, his underwear was a nonstarter. And as for his BVD preferences, she wouldn't have been surprised if he slept in his birthday suit. Or maybe she just hoped that was the case.

One thing was clear. The man was a hell of a chef. Tonight's *coq au vin* was so good Mr. Little had sent his regards to the chef. The man had actually been smiling with satisfaction as he'd pushed back his chair at the end of the meal. Even his wife seemed to relax as if the pin was back in the grenade.

Their other diners had similar reactions. Mr. and Mrs. Barclay came in from town for their anniversary dinner and commented that Chuck's skills had dramatically improved. When Frankie told them there was a new chef who'd come from New York, they'd been suitably impressed. And given Mrs. Barclay's penchant for talking, it was a good bet phones would be ringing all around Saranac Lake with the news. Thank God.

As she got to the head of the stairs, Frankie was wishing that someone else could floss and brush her teeth for her when Nate stepped out of the bathroom.

Not exactly the someone she was looking for, she thought.

He'd changed into a Boston Red Sox T-shirt and had a towel draped around his neck. His smile was casual. His eyes were not.

"I thought you'd never come upstairs," he said, as if he'd been waiting for her.

She began to struggle for words, especially as his smile widened. Being tongue-tied was a new one for her, but around him, she was getting used to it. Tragically.

"You work too hard, Frances. Good night." He turned away and went down to his room.

She felt as if she'd been left behind, somehow.

Which was crazy, she told herself. You couldn't be left if you were in your own home. And the person in question was just across the hall. And you didn't want to be with him, anyway.

Oh, hell, she thought, shutting herself in the bathroom. She was still muttering under her breath when she came back out, turned off the hall light, and headed for her room.

Nate's door was open and she paused in front of it. To do otherwise would have required a disciplined purpose she seemed to have left downstairs in her office.

He was sitting up in bed, back against the wall, legs

kicked out. A book was open on his lap and he looked up from it with a grin as if he'd set a trap that had worked. That spider/fly parlor saying flared in her head and she was about to mutter a quick good-night when his hand crept to the side of his neck and he scratched.

"Didn't you put calamine on that?" She looked over at the bag that she'd put on his dresser. It was unopened.

"No. I forgot."

Frankie went over and took out the pink bottle. "Put this on and the itching won't keep you up all night."

But when she held the lotion out to him, he merely tilted his neck.

"Would you mind doing the honors? I have a feeling you'll do a better job."

"I'm not a nurse."

"And we're not really talking about brain surgery here, are we?" He smiled more widely and she noticed that one of his front teeth had a very good cap on it. "Please?"

Grabbing a couple of tissues from a box, she cracked open the bottle and tipped it over. Gently, she dabbed his skin with the chalky pink lotion.

"Mmm." The sound he made was something between a moan and a sigh. He closed his eyes and leaned towards her. "That feels great."

She paused, thinking she wished he wouldn't say anything. And no more noises, either, *please.*

"Are you finished already?" he asked. His voice was a low growl, husky and deep. She imagined what it would sound like in her ear when he kissed her on the neck.

"Ah, no."

Frankie snapped into action, going back and forth between the bottle and the inflamed blisters until the job was done. When she pulled away, he opened his eyes.

"Thanks."

"It doesn't look like it's spreading." She tossed the tissue into the trash can across the room and put the cap on the bottle.

"Good shot." He was looking at her, with speculation in his eyes. "You mind if I ask how old you are?"

"Yes, but I have nothing to hide. I'm thirty-one."

"And how long have you been running this place?"

She hesitated, not wanting to get into particulars with him. His questions about her past had disturbed her earlier in the day. At night, alone with him, they felt even more intrusive.

She turned away and headed for the hall, thinking there was no way the conversation could continue with her out of the room.

"Good night, Nate."

"Wait—"

She shut her door on his question and the searching look on his handsome face but a moment later, she heard a soft knock. Pivoting around, she grabbed the knob and opened wide, shooting him the level stare that usually got her what she wanted from people.

Which was to be left alone.

"Yes?"

He smiled, utterly impervious to her warning signals. "I don't mean to pry."

"Yes, you do."

Nate smiled. "You're very blunt. I like that in a woman."

"It's a handy trait to have. Especially if you're being harassed."

"Is that really what you think I'm doing?"

She looked down. He put her on edge and she resented it, but not enough to keep up the lie she'd started.

"I just don't understand why," she said softly. "I'm not..."

She pushed her hair back as if the gesture of exposing her face would explain what she didn't want to put into words. It was hard to say she was plain, even though it was a truth she'd come to accept.

He reached out, cupping her chin gently. "Not what?"

She felt him taking off her glasses. With nothing to hide her eyes, she felt as naked as if she'd left all her clothes in the bathroom.

"Not what?" he repeated.

"Like Joy." It was as close as she could come.

"I know." He stroked her cheek with the pad of his thumb.

"So why are you pretending that you find me so interesting?"

He leaned in close and she felt his lips brush against her cheek as he spoke. "I'm not pretending."

She thought about putting her arms around his neck and pulling him into her bedroom. But then she pictured the morning after. The awkwardness because she'd hope it was a beginning and not an ending. The strained politeness because he'd gotten what he'd wanted and now had to pretend to be nice so he didn't feel like a complete ass. She'd done that god-awful dance once before and the only thing remotely bearable about it then had been the fact that the guy was from out of town. Nate worked for her. Was supposed to be at White Caps for the whole summer. The last thing she wanted was to be reminded daily of another bad decision when it came to men. She was already pretending everything was fine with the business around her family. Did she really want to have to put on an act about her love life, too?

She stared up into his eyes and tried to read the future in the flecks of green and gold.

Pulling back, she reached for her glasses and thought there was a damn fine line between self-preservation and cowardice. "I think it's best that we not take things any further."

"I'm sure you're right."

"Good. I'm glad we agree."

"We don't." He smiled slowly. "What's life without a little excitement? Risk?"

Easy for him to say.

She pointed across the room, trying to ignore his charm the same way he disregarded her ire. "You want a charge? There's an electrical socket over there. I'm sure we can find something metal for you to stick into it."

He was laughing as he grabbed her hand and put it on his heart. "And if I go into cardiac arrest, will you revive me?"

"I'd call 911. And pray that two men with garlic breath come to save you."

She tried to turn away but he held on. "I just want to know one more thing."

"Somehow I doubt that." She firmly removed her hand and crossed her arms over her chest.

"When was the last time you went out on a date?"

"Do you ever give up?" She started to shut the door.

"You didn't answer my question," he said, putting his body in the way.

"Why do I have to?"

"It's generally considered polite."

"Even if someone's being nosy?"

"I'm not nosy. I have a reason for wanting to know. Nosy is much more gratuitous."

"Look, you're being paid to cook here. That's it. So unless you've got questions about supplies or the kitchen, everything else is none of your business."

His eyebrow cocked.

"You're one tough lady, aren't you?" He was talking to himself, his eyes narrowed, assessing.

Frankie had to laugh. "Right now, I'm tired. My feet hurt. I just want to go to sleep. If that's your version of tough, you've nailed me dead to rights, but I think you need to check the dictionary. The rest of the world thinks the word means something else."

She pushed at him, but it was like trying to budge a parked car.

"Are you going to answer my question?"

"Fine. Sure." She kicked up her chin. "My life's one long party. Calendar's so packed I have the men come with name tags otherwise I forget who they are. Yippee."

"Well, if you can fit it in, how'd you like to go out somewhere with me?" He smiled casually, but she wasn't fooled. His eyes had that purposeful look in them she was beginning to recognize all too well.

She couldn't believe she'd mistaken him for an aimless drifter. The guy didn't have a wayward bone in his body.

"Hell," she murmured.

"Not exactly the response I was hoping for. Doesn't answer the question, either."

"I just have a feeling that's where I'm headed if I get involved with you," she said, pulling away.

"Why's that?"

"Good night, Nate."

"I'm not going to give up, you know."

"Do you always come on this strong?"

He traced her lips with his eyes, in what was apparently becoming a habit for him. "When I find something I want, absolutely."

"Then it's going to be a long, lonely summer for you."

This time, he let her shut the door.

Leaning back against the panels, she closed her eyes and let herself enjoy a stolen moment of insanity. She imagined that instead of shutting him out, she'd let him come in. Let him take off her clothes and lay her down on the bed—

"It's going to be good between us." Nate's voice came through the wood, right next to her ear. "I promise you."

Frankie jumped like she was the one with a finger in the socket. She stuck her head out in the hall, ready to tell him to go back to his room, but his door was just clicking into place.

So it was hard to know if he'd meant her to hear him or not. And she had to wonder whether the words he'd spoken were an empty entreaty or a vow.

Getting into bed, she pondered the two possibilities until all she thought about was the dark, starving expression on his face when he'd stared at her. The image was inescapable and her body temperature soared. Smoldering, she proceeded to kick off her comforter, her blanket and her socks. She opened the window a little further and then got the box fan out of the closet. She put it on her bedside table and tuned it up so it blew great gusts over her skin.

She'd probably have had better luck if she'd just put her head down on her desk and slept in her office. She might have woken up with a paper clip or two stuck to her forehead, but surely that would have been better than trying to find REM sleep in a wind tunnel.

Nate got up with the sun, pulled on an old pair of cut-off jeans and went looking for a ladder. He wasn't interested in the step variety he'd run into the day before in the pantry. He was looking for the real deal, the house painter's kind, the dual layer, extendomatic, break-your-head, trip-to-the-Emergency-Room special. The Big Daddy of ladders.

And White Caps being what it was, he was confident he'd find one somewhere. He'd learned in the past forty-eight hours that the barn and the house's cellar were repositories for all manner of things. You had to wonder how a WWI bazooka, a gin distillery and a printing press came to be housed under the same roof.

Then again, maybe that did make sense.

It took twenty minutes and a brush with a spider the size of his head to find the ladder of his dreams. Grabbing a screwdriver from a toolbox, he took the aluminum nightmare over to the spot where he and Frankie had argued over lawn mowing duties. Tipping it up, he extended the thing as quietly as he could, but it was like whispering in church. The sounds were amplified by the silence around him and he felt like he was putting a jackhammer to the side of the house instead of carefully inching the rungs up to the broken gutter.

He was supposed to be helping Frankie, not tuning Mr. Little up for another explosion she'd have to smooth over. And Nate could have waited until people were awake, but he knew she would insist on helping him or doing it herself so he was willing to take the risk.

He surveyed the ladder placement with satisfaction, put his foot on the first rung, and started climbing. He was about halfway up when his fear of heights checked in with a heave-ho of his stomach. Refusing to let an irrational anxiety deter him, he got through the nausea by focusing on his hands as they gripped and regripped.

When he got up to the gutter, he was relieved to discover he probably could solve the problem. It wouldn't be as efficient or pretty as the turnaround he'd preformed on the chicken that first night in Frankie's kitchen. But at least he could reattach the holder-thing that kept the gutter close to the house.

The sound of a fan had been droning while he'd been climbing and now he was curious. Going down a few rungs and leaning to one side, so that he could look into an open window, he realized he was staring into Frankie's bedroom. And then he saw her.

She was laying on her back in bed, an arm and a leg hanging off one side and the covers on the floor. She was resplendent. In the process of flopping around, her shirt had ridden up, exposing one perfect breast and her flat stomach. His eyes traced her skin and lingered on her white cotton panties.

Which were somehow sexier than the lace and satin numbers he'd seen on other women.

Staring into her room, struck dumb by attraction, knowing that he was a Peeping Tom and feeling badly about it, he hoped like hell she didn't wake up. But sure enough, it was about then that Frankie started fidgeting in her sleep.

Not about to get caught, Nate took a quick step back into thin air.

Frankie was awoken by a howling noise and she shot out of bed. The next thing she heard was the sound of something like a tree hitting the side of the house right outside her window.

She ran across the room, threw up the screen.

And looked into Nate's horrified face.

"What the hell—" she stuttered.

"Am I doing up here?" He was hugging the ladder he was on. "I'm trying to fix the gutter." Moving gingerly, he reached into the pocket of his cutoffs and took out a screwdriver. "See?"

"But why?"

"I thought it was better than you having to do it." He was clearly trying to recover from scaring himself half to death and determined not to show it. The smile he gave her was the same easy, wide one he used on the ground.

But his face was the color of pea soup.

"And this is because you're so scary brilliant with the Mr. Fix-It stuff?" she chided gently.

"All I need to do is just screw in that thing. Up. There." He let go of the ladder long enough to gesture with the tool and push at the gutter. Two seconds later both hands were back on the rungs.

He was scared of heights, she realized. And doing his damnedest not to show it.

"Why don't we get you down from there?"

"Naw, don't worry about me. I'm fine. I'll just finish what I started." But then he made the mistake of looking down and squeezed his eyes shut. "Ah, Jesus."

"Nate?" He opened one eye. "I really think you should get down on the ground."

"I can see your point."

But he didn't move.

"Why don't you just try one rung down from where you are. I'm right here. I'll talk you through it."

"I'm fine."

"You're scared of heights and you're stuck twenty-five feet up in the air. I don't think I'd call that fine."

"I'm not scared of anything."

Tell that to your adrenal gland, she thought.

Frankie sat on the windowsill and considered the options for helping him down. Distraction. That was what he needed. Distraction and a little motivation.

The solution was obvious. Enticing. Dangerous.

"So you can go back inside," he was saying to her. "I'm just going to catch my breath for a sec and then—"

"Nate?"

"Hmm?" It was a pleasant enough noise. He didn't open his eyes, though.

"I have a feeling that if I leave you here, you're still going to be on this ladder at noontime."

"Untrue."

Could she really do this, she wondered.

· Frankie leaned out and put a hand on his cheek. It was clammy, as if he had a fever.

Her touch got his attention. His lids flipped open.

She refused to think about what she was about to do. She just leaned forward and pressed her lips to his firmly. A shocked hiss come out of his mouth as she pulled back.

"You're a sick woman," he said softly. "Why do you

wait until I'm completely freaked out and stuck on the side of your house before you'll kiss me?"

"Shhh." She dipped back down and this time he was ready for her. His lips responded instantly, moving against hers. His tongue snuck out and the kiss deepened.

God, he felt good.

Frankie buried her hand in his hair, feeling the lush texture. He kissed like a real man, she thought. Hungry, hot, demanding.

There was a scraping noise as the ladder shifted against the siding and they broke apart sharply.

Ho, boy. The idea was to get him down to the ground in one piece. Not kiss him into a dead fall.

"There's more where that came from, Nate. But only when you can take me into your arms properly." Her voice was shaky. From the scare. From the heat between them. From the fact that she didn't mean what she said. She just wanted a way to get him back on the ground.

Nate, however, obviously took her at her word. He started down that ladder like he'd been trained by a fireman.

That was when she realized she was halfway out her bedroom window, wearing nothing but a T-shirt and panties, having kissed a man for the first time in…heck, she couldn't count that high this early in the morning.

Frankie threw on a pair of jeans and rushed downstairs, hoping like hell he didn't get stuck again. She rounded the corner and was relieved to see that he was safe, on the ground.

But coming at her with an unmistakable look of intention.

She put her hands up. "I'm really glad you got down—"

"Come over here."

"Now, look, we just needed to get you—"

"A promise is a promise."

Nate marched up to her, put his hands on either side of her face and kissed her long and slow. His body was warm against hers, and as he pushed her back against the house, she couldn't remember exactly why it was wrong to be with him.

Something about leaving, the end of the summer—ah, who the hell cared, she thought.

Her hands crept up his shoulders and around the back of his neck and she held on to him. He smelled like Ivory soap and outdoors, but she would have taken him dirty and sweaty, too.

"Much better on the ground," he murmured.

Frankie slowly opened her eyes. "I'm not sure I'm standing up anymore, to tell you the truth."

He smiled with satisfaction. "You want to go upstairs?"

"Yes—no. No, I—" She thought about stepping away but her feet refused to respond.

Probably because her size eight and a halfs knew she wasn't really serious about wanting to put some space between her body and Nate's.

He kissed her lightly and tucked a piece of hair behind her ear. "I take that back. How about we go a little more slowly. Let's go out tonight after we close. Just the two of us."

It was weird, but the tempting invitation made reality come back. Maybe because she pictured herself taking him into town and having people watch them together. In a small community, there wasn't much to do except gossip. And the conclusions that would be drawn, namely that she was sleeping with her new chef, wouldn't help her or her business.

But that wasn't the only reason to not go any further with him.

Frankie pulled back and then stepped away.

"Actually, I think we should stop."

He groaned deep in his throat. "Why?"

"Because I like you," she muttered. Before he could ask her to elaborate, she put her hand up. "Look, you're leaving at the end of the summer and nothing is going to change that. I've got too much self-respect to be some man's little diversion and I'm not interested in using you in that way, either."

His hazel eyes burned as he stared at her. "Fine, but it may not be that easy."

And with that, he turned and headed back for the ladder.

"What's that supposed to mean?" she demanded, going after him.

He just shrugged and put his foot on the bottom rung. "You're assuming we have a choice."

She watched him take a deep breath, and with his eyes fixated on the gutter, begin to steadily climb back up the side of the house.

Chapter Seven

A week later, she still couldn't get that kiss out of her mind.

Although she took a lot of pride in spanking down Nate's fatalistic attitude. No matter how attractive he was, or how good he'd felt, she'd managed to not jump his bones. She felt like a chronic dieter who'd made it through a Lindt store without buckling.

Restraint came at a cost, however.

Frankie put her head down on her desk. It was utterly exhausting trying to convince her body that it didn't actually want to be invaded by his.

And her nerves were shot. Whenever she was in the same room with Nate, she wanted to jump out of her skin. She kept expecting him to bring up what had happened or try it again, but he was playing it cool.

And naturally, the space he gave her meant she thought about him constantly.

The nights were the worst. She made a point to go up to bed before him, reinforcing the hands-off message with her closed door. It was a good, stalwart plan, in theory. The trouble was, when she heard him coming down the hall, she kept wishing he'd ignore the signal. She wanted him to knock, probably just so that she could turn him down again. Which was crazy and a little cruel, but somehow drawing the boundaries would make her feel more in control.

As it was, she had to listen to the shower going while imagining what he looked like naked and running a bar of her soap over all of those muscles.

Seeing him in the kitchen was an exercise in self-torment, too, even though he was fully clothed. It was next to impossible for her not to get caught up in watching him cook. You wouldn't figure some man facing off ten pounds of root vegetables with a paring knife would be so damned attractive.

But she could watch him peel potatoes for hours.

He had beautiful hands. Long, strong fingers and wide palms. His forearms were thick and marked with veins and she loved to watch the tendons and muscles shift as he worked.

God, she was pathetic.

But that was what self-imposed sexual frustration could do to a girl.

In an effort to release some stress, she'd made twenty jars of jam this afternoon. Nate had thought she'd lost her mind when she'd pushed him away from the stove, pulled a stew vat over a flame and proceeded to pitch in about a thousand strawberries and enough sugar to put the city of Albany into a diabetic coma.

The excess was absurd, but she'd give the stuff away to guests as they left. And at least she'd managed to keep her hands off him for another day.

Of course, she'd also wiped out the strawberry census in Saranac for the time being. But there were always blueberries. And raspberries. And rhubarb.

Hell, she could probably make jam out of grass if she ran out of options.

The phone rang and she jumped. She cleared her throat before picking up, just in case her fantasy life had made her hoarse.

"Yes, we have rooms available," she said, cradling the receiver between her ear and shoulder. She changed screens on the computer. "This weekend I can offer you a lake-facing suite for two nights. No, I'm sorry, the Lincoln Bedroom is booked. Of course, we love children."

After she took the man's credit card information, she referred him to their Web site for directions. "And may I ask where you heard of us?"

She was still surprised when she hung up the phone. Mr. Little had evidently been impressed enough by the food to give a recommendation to a friend of his. Which meant for the first time this season, they were full for the coming weekend.

Joy stuck her head in the door. "Plumber's back again. He's got the replacement part and he's going to need to work in here."

Thank God. The day after the deluge, he'd managed to patch the slow drip that had caused water to accumulate in the ceiling, but it had been a short-term solution.

With any luck, a new valve would take care of the problem and she could get a sheet rocker in to seal up the rafters.

As the guy came in with his toolbox, Frankie figured she'd spend some time in the garden, weeding. She changed into ratty shorts and was heading out to the raggedy patch when a Cadillac pulled up. Mike Roy got out and so did a tall, dark-haired man. Both were dressed casually, although the stranger seemed somewhat regal in his linen pants and polo shirt.

Great timing for Mike to show up, she thought, looking down at her clothes. She was doing an excellent impression of a bag lady.

Frustration surged. They'd been playing phone tag all week and she was finally set to see him in his office on Monday. She'd been looking forward to making a professional presentation of her finances and reassuring him that she was going to meet her obligations. Now, that image was going to be harder to project.

Why hadn't he called, she groaned. She would have changed.

Mike waved and then smiled, his bearded cheeks stretching wide at something the man next to him said. "Hey, Frankie. We just came from the airport and I figured I'd take a chance that you'd be here. Karl Graves, meet Frances Moorehouse."

As she shook hands, she could feel herself being assessed. The man's grip was strong, his eyes direct, his smile on the chilly side.

"I apologize for the intrusion," Graves said, his English accent clipping the words into place. "But may we trouble you for a tour?"

"Certainly." She smiled at Mike, but he was looking

at his car keys while he turned them over in his hand. "Well, let's go. Are you thinking of summering here?"

Because the Englishman didn't look like the year-round type. Not in the slightest.

"Perhaps." Unlike Mike, the man's eyes were all over White Caps. "I live in London but the base of my business is moving to the States."

"What do you do?"

"I own some hotels."

She laughed ruefully. "So you know what it's like to deal with guests and their demands."

"Yes, I know something of it."

Mike hung back as she gave the tour. She started with the rooms of the first floor and Graves seemed legitimately impressed by the hand-carved moldings around the high ceilings and the wide-planked cherry floors. And he knew his stuff when it came to architecture. He talked intelligently about the Federal period and the house's infamous architect, Thomas Crane.

"It's unusual to see a Crane this far north," Graves said as they went upstairs. The man's hand lingered on the thick mahogany balustrade when they reached the landing. "Tell me, do you still have the original plans?"

"There are two sets. One is here. The other is in the National Gallery in D.C." She took a left at the top of the stairs and went lake-side. "Lincoln's bedroom is over here. He spent three nights with Charles Moorehouse the Third in August of 1859 just prior to announcing his candidacy. Lincoln's thank-you note is framed and hanging on the wall. In it, he mentions the view and the island which you can see to the north—"

She opened the door and stopped dead. Her grandmother was kneeling on the floor, swinging a butcher's knife over her head. Dressed in a peach gown, she was sprinkled with plaster dust and gravely serious.

"Grand-Em!"

Frankie rushed forward as her grandmother heaved her arms and buried the knife in the wall. Before Grand-Em could lift the thing again, Frankie disarmed her.

"I beg your pardon," was the indignant response. "Give that back!"

"What are you doing?"

"That's none of your concern. This is my room. I shall do what I wish in it."

What she wished, evidently, was to make one hell of a hole in the wall, and for a frail woman of eighty, she had a good start on the job. There was a four-inch cavity in the plaster and Frankie could see through to the wall joists.

"Maybe we should leave you two alone," Mike said.

Grand-Em looked over at him. With fragile dignity, she pushed a length of white hair back from her face and assumed an expectant look, as if she were waiting to be properly introduced. In her day, ladies did not speak to persons unknown and waited for someone else to make acquaintances.

Which gave Frankie a shot at getting the men out of the way.

"Thank you, Mike," she said, getting to her feet. "Please feel free to look around. I'll meet you both on the lawn in about ten minutes."

"Take however long you need," the banker said.

Frankie shut the door behind them and hid the knife in the top drawer of the dresser. She wished she could have spared her grandmother the shocked curiosity on their faces, although she couldn't really blame Mike or that Graves man for being spellbound. The sad reality was that Grand-Em looked out of her mind, sitting on the floor in an ancient, faded dress with dust in her frizzy white hair and a knife over her head aimed at the wall.

As Frankie went back across the room, her eye caught an old, grainy photograph of her grandmother. She'd been in her early twenties and was sitting in an Adirondack guide boat on the lake, holding a parasol in one hand. Long ago, people had visited White Caps just to see if the rumors of her beauty were lies and exaggerations. Back then, she'd been talked about in whispers for things a woman wanted to be known for. Not because she was old and crazy.

Grand-Em reached forward, starting to paw the plaster with her bare hands, and Frankie quickly stilled the knobby fingers. Her grandmother's skin felt dry and flimsy and there were red spots that had been rubbed raw by the knife handle.

"What's going on?" Frankie asked gently.

Grand-Em's sparse brows sunk low over her milky blue eyes. Smoothing the palms of her grandmother's hands, Frankie asked again, "What were you doing?"

Grand-Em looked at the wall. "I can't seem to find it."

"What are you looking for?"

"My ring."

"Which one?"

"My first engagement ring."

Frankie turned over the old hands and touched the little diamond in the plain gold setting. "But it's right here. Right where it should be."

"No, no, my first one. The one that Arthur Phillip Garrison gave me."

"Grand-Em, you were never engaged to someone named Garrison."

"True. But he asked me to marry him. In 1941. I told him no because I found him not exactly trustworthy, but he was quite sure of himself and left the ring with me. I had to hide it from Father because he would have made me marry him. Poor Arthur. He died not long afterward. I kept the stone because it was announced in his obituary that he was engaged to another woman. Given everything she was dealing with, I figured she wouldn't have wanted to know about me."

Frankie shook her head. If the story had come out even two years before, she might have been tempted to believe it. But Grand-Em had started to get her life's history mixed up, assigning events to her own past that were borrowed from the lives of others. Last week, she'd declared that her husband had been elected to the Senate and that she'd lived in Washington, D.C. on Pennsylvania Avenue. This was after she'd seen a biography on R.F.K.

God only knew who Arthur Garrison was or where she'd picked his name up.

"Grand-Em, why don't we go find Joy?"

"No. No. I must finish what I started. I hid the ring from Father in the wall."

Frankie gently tugged on her arm. "Come on, now—"

"I will *not!*" Her grandmother pulled free. "This is my room."

"This is a guest room. Your room is in the back of the house."

Grand-Em's eyes popped wide open as hysteria reddened her pale cheeks and tightened her hands into fists. "Are you suggesting I live with the staff?"

Frankie tried to stay calm. "Don't you remember—" Now that was a stupid thing to say. "Let's go find Joy."

"I have work to do here."

"There's nothing in the wall, Grand-Em. There's no ring except the one on your finger."

"Are you suggesting I'm crazy?" she said softly.

"No, I—"

"You're going to put me away! You're going to let them take me!"

Frankie tried to keep her voice level. "No. Never. This is your home."

"I'm not going to get shut away like some insane person!"

With a violent lurch, Grand-Em shot to her feet but she got caught in the skirts of her dress and pitched forward at an alarming angle. She let out a cry and Frankie lunged forward, grabbing her just before her forehead made contact with a marble-topped bed stand. But instead of feeling saved, Grand-Em obviously assumed she'd been captured because she fought harder. Frankie was able to hold her so that she couldn't hurt herself, but took a lot of kicks in the shins before the struggling finally stopped. When Grand-Em fell still, she let out a soft sob.

"I promise to be better. I just don't want to go," she moaned. "Please don't send me away. I am lost…even when I am home. What will happen if I am somewhere unknown?"

Frankie held her tightly, feeling the small body underneath the yards of old silk. "I promise. I promise you won't have to go away. Please don't worry."

Grand-Em put her hands to her face, as if trying to compose herself. She was wheezing raggedly, her chest moving in and out like a bird's.

"Let's sit down," Frankie said. She helped Grand-Em up to the bed and eyed the phone on the stand, wondering where Joy was. At times like this, Frankie wished she had her sister's way with their grand-mother. Maybe if Joy had been the one to walk in, she could have stopped Grand-Em without spurring an attack.

Frankie knelt down and regarded her grandmother with concern. Grand-Em was still shaking and gasping for air. It could have just been the remnants of the panic attack, but maybe it was the harbinger of something more dangerous.

"Are you having trouble breathing? Does your head hurt?"

Grand-Em looked down and a tear rolled down her hollow cheek.

"Shhh." Frankie stroked her grandmother's white hair, smoothing the waves. "Let's just catch our breath for a moment."

When the shaking stopped, Frankie asked whether she was feeling better and got no response. Leaning forward, she put her face in the line of her grandmother's vision. "How are you feeling?"

Grand-Em blinked and then narrowed her eyes. She reached out and touched Frankie's face. "I know you. You're Frances. My granddaughter."

Frankie grabbed the frail hand, pressing it urgently into her cheek. "Yes, yes, I'm Frances."

The brief periods of lucidity never lasted long, so what needed to be said had to be spoken fast and clearly. It had been over a year since the last time Grand-Em had recognized anyone. Even Joy.

"Grand-Em, listen to me. We're not going to send

you away. Not ever. We love you. You're safe." Frankie couldn't say it enough. "You're safe. You will never end up in an institution."

Grand-Em's eyes were full of sorrow. "But of course I shall. Someday you will have to send me away and you must know that it is okay. Every once in a while I remember who I was and that tells me how far gone I truly am."

Frankie reached for the phone. She kept hold of her grandmother's eyes as if that could keep her tethered to reality long enough for Joy to get upstairs.

"Joy, come quickly. I'm in the Lincoln bedroom."

"Joy is here? How lovely." Grand-Em looked down at herself and then over at the hole. "What a mess. Who could have done—oh, it was me, wasn't it." Distress flared and then was resolved. "I was looking for my ring. Because someone is getting married."

Demented purpose started to replace the clarity and Frankie put herself right in her grandmother's face. "Grand-Em. Look at me. Stay with me. Don't you go yet, do you hear me?"

Grand-Em laughed, a short burst of breath that left her lips in a smile. "Your sister and I may look alike, but you and I, we share the same heart. We are both the fighting kind, aren't we? That was why I married your grandfather even though Father hated it. I married a gardener for love and I was never sorry."

Joy burst through the door. "What's wrong?"

Grand-Em clapped her hands triumphantly. "She is getting married and needs my ring. Now, if I can just get back to what I was doing…."

Frankie could only shake her head as her sister took in the hole in the wall and all the plaster mess.

"When is your ceremony?" Grand-Em asked as Joy sat beside her.

"But I'm not getting married," Joy said tenderly. "Besides, what would Grand-dad think if someone else were to wear your ring? I don't think he'd like that at all."

"No, not this one. The one Arthur Phillip Garrison gave to me in 1941…."

Frankie watched as their grandmother drifted back out into the lake of madness.

"She came out of it," Frankie whispered to Joy. "I didn't want you to miss the opportunity."

Thank you, Joy mouthed while nodding at Grand-Em. "Well, Arthur Garrison must have been handsome. Why don't we go to your room and change? I just finished ironing your pale yellow gown and I think it would be perfect for a sunny day like today, don't you?"

As her sister led Grand-Em out of the room, Frankie looked out a window and saw Mike Roy and that Graves man down by the lakeshore. Mike was pointing up, behind the house, towards the mountain. Before she went to join them, she moved the dresser over next to the bed and put the lamp on top. It was a great way to cover the hole without having to pay someone to fix it.

An hour later, Frankie watched Mike and the Englishman disappear down the driveway. She really wished she could erase their whole visit and start all over again.

When the screen door slapped shut behind her, she knew who it was without turning around.

"So who was that guy with the beard?" Nate walked up to her, a paper bag in his hands. His smile was big and easy, as if the whole kiss-on-the-ladder, spurned-date thing hadn't happened.

"A friend." Because after all Mike Roy had done for her, he seemed more than a banker. "Where are you headed?"

"Up the mountain for lunch. You want to join me?" He joggled the bag. "Got enough for two in here."

She opened her mouth to say no, but thought of the plumber in her office and the jungle of weeds in the garden. The last thing she wanted was to be alone with her thoughts because replaying the scene upstairs would be the inevitable result. Besides, it had been a long time since she'd been up the mountain and some physical exercise sounded like a good way to blow off steam.

Nate lowered his voice. "And don't worry about the height phobia thing. That's only planes, balconies and bridges. Well, ladders, too, evidently. Otherwise, I'm one tough character." He pounded his chest. "All man."

Frankie smiled up at him. "Then come on, Tarzan. Let's hit the trail."

As they started out, she thought it was hard not to be impressed by the guy. In spite of his fear of heights, he'd managed to fix the gutter after all. Still, she hoped if he ended up channeling his inner handyman again, he'd keep to the ground.

Frankie led him down the driveway and across Route 22. The way up the mountain started with a rough road that had a bright orange "No Trespassing" sign right next to it. It was hard to know whether the notice functioned as a deterrent or merely helped tourists find their way, but Frankie had never minded if people wanted to hike the trail.

"Can you drive all the way up?" Nate asked as they each settled into one of the grooves in the road.

"Only part way."

The dark forest surrounded them, the trees a cool, protective shield, the ferns and grasses a lovely green carpet. The air smelled like pine and earth and she felt the tension leave her body.

Just as they hit the trail proper, the road broke off to the right. Nate stopped while she went ahead.

"What's over here?"

"The graveyard. But there's not much to see."

He started down the road.

"Nate? Let's just keep going, okay? Nate?"

There was no answer, just the sound of his boots cracking an occasional stick, so she cursed and went after him. When she came up to the familiar stone py-lons and the gate that was made out of unshucked cedar branches in the Adirondack style, she stopped. The barrier kept the cars out although pedestrians could easily walk around it and go inside, as Nate had. The only time the heavy arm was swung open was for burials or regular maintenance and there was an old, ratty chain with a fresh Master lock hanging at one side.

Putting her hands on the top rail, she felt the rough scratch of the bark against her palms. Ahead, in a flat grassy plain, there were some twenty gray slate head-stones, lined up in rows. There were no showy angels or Christ figures, no temple-like artifices. Just stones marking when people had checked in and out. Frankie knew she would be buried there, and so would her brother and sister and Grand-Em, of course. But after that, who else would? She wasn't in a big hurry to get married and start a family and neither was Alex. Who knew what Joy would do.

Nate paused in front of a grave. "This one is dated 1827. Is it the earliest?"

"No. That was Charles Moorehouse's second son, Edward. The first, Charles, Jr., died in infancy—1811."

He touched the weathered, lichen-covered slab. "Edward died young. Fifteen, was he?"

She nodded and Nate moved on. He seemed to take care not to step on the ground in front of the stones, as if he didn't want to trample on the dead. She didn't know, though, whether the coffins had been buried in front of or behind the markers. When her grandfather had died, she'd been too young to remember much of anything. And when her parents had been laid to rest, she'd been down at the house. The day she'd finally gone up to see where they'd been buried, some two years later, the grass had all grown in.

She supposed that had been the last time she'd walked around the gate.

A part of her wanted to join Nate, she realized. To wander around, look at the inscriptions, remember faces from black-and-white pictures that hung on the walls or were protected in leather bound albums. But she knew sooner or later she would come to two headstones that would make her hurt so she stayed away from all of them.

Her parents had died in a May storm out on the lake, and the beautiful spring day when they'd been buried was a memory clear enough to have Frankie coughing away a lump in her throat. The sun had been thoughtlessly bright, the sky a cruel and lovely blue. The birds had been in the trees and there had been buds everywhere you looked. Worst of all, there had been boats out on the lake, skimming across docile waves. Watching them go by, she'd wondered why some lives got to go on while others were stopped in the middle.

Right before the service, Frankie had told Joy and Alex that she had to watch over the B & B, and would stay at the house. It hadn't been the whole truth and she'd had a feeling they knew it. The thing was, she'd been afraid of making a fool of herself by bursting into tears. Up until the day of the burials, she'd only had one crying jag. It had kicked off when she'd opened the back door that terrible night and found two local cops on the other side. The men were standing in the rain with their hats off, looking at their shoes. Her father had been gone in the storm for two hours by then, her mother for a little over an hour.

She'd sobbed through the awkward words of sympathy they'd offered and she'd thought the crying would never stop, but then Joy had come downstairs. Frankie could never forget the expression on her sister's face as the girl had taken in the scene. She'd been stone-cold terrified, and when she'd asked whether she still had a family, Frankie had made a vow. Wiping her eyes, she'd decided her sister was not going to grow up without a parent. Frankie had no idea how to be one, but she figured the first rule of thumb was no more crying. Tears meant you were scared and the last thing a teenager needed was a caregiver who was falling apart.

Frankie had intended to go to the memorial service, she really had. But then Alex had finally showed up and that meant Joy had someone to stand next to and Frankie had an out. She'd been worried about staying strong through the service, picturing herself weeping and having to be escorted away by some distant, caring relative. In front of Joy. Or God, maybe it would have been even worse. She'd easily been able to imagine throwing herself on her father's coffin and pounding on it as if she could get his attention somehow.

She thought about doing that, still.

And what would she say to him? She was ashamed of the truth. The first thing out of her mouth wouldn't be *I love you.* It would be more along the lines of *What the* hell *did you think you were doing when you headed out on the lake in that storm in a half-restored boat? And Didn't you know she would come after you, you selfish bastard?*

"Someone's been up here."

Frankie braced herself and looked over at the two newest graves, which weren't new anymore. Ten years had brought a thick thatch of grass around her parents' headstones and some moss to the sides of the markers. The tree, which had been planted to shade their resting places, a hearty hemlock that Frankie had been assured would survive the harsh winters, was now six feet tall. At its base was a small bouquet on the ground and the flowers were from White Caps' garden. No doubt Joy had come up recently for a visit.

Frankie stared hard at the lilacs. She would have liked to show her grief in such an acceptable, dignified way. She wanted to mourn with quiet, soul-felt love. But a decade later she wasn't anymore capable of such convention than she would have been the day they'd been buried. Soldiering on had put the trauma in cold storage, so on those rare occasions she let herself think of the past, the emotions were as raw as ever.

She heard a stick snap and focused her eyes. Nate

had come over to her although she hadn't sensed him moving.

"You want to go?" he asked.

"I want to be like my sister," she blurted. "Putting down pretty flowers. Talking to their headstones."

Nate covered her hand with one of his. His eyes were grave and tender. "You must miss them, still."

"I curse him and hate myself for it. Missing them would be a relief." She turned and walked away. "Let's head on up the trail."

Chapter Eight

From his perch on the mountain's summit, Nate had a good look at Frankie. She was standing on a rock ledge in front of him, surveying the strip of lake that was far below. Her hands were on her hips and the wind was blowing her hair around, pulling strands out of her ponytail.

It had been a mistake to go to the graveyard, he thought.

"Beautiful view," he said.

"Isn't it." Her words were carried back to him on the wind.

Their pace up the mountain had been a bruising one. She was a steady, sure hiker, and she hadn't slowed down even through the hardest parts of the trail. Going over a rock face, scurrying up the messy remnants of a mudslide, traversing a river or a fallen tree, she just kept pressing on.

"You want to eat?" he asked, picking up the bag and unrolling the top.

She looked at him over her shoulder. "Good idea. I'm hungry."

Nate fell still. He could barely see her face in the swirl of hair, but he could feel her eyes on him. She had a smudge of dirt on the side of her neck and her T-shirt had come untucked from her shorts. There was mud on her calves and her socks.

And she was the loveliest woman he'd ever seen.

Frankie walked over to him. "What did you bring us?"

Blinking twice, he felt his body shift in his skin, if that was possible, and then a wave of something like nausea hit his belly. He thought about altitude sickness, but that was what you got in the Himalayas. Not the Adirondacks.

She sat down beside him, stretching her legs out next to his and leaning back on her hands. She frowned. "Are you okay? Is the height bothering you?"

It wasn't the height. He'd surprised himself, that was all.

He'd always assumed that at the age of thirty-eight, there were very few firsts left in his life. First root canal, sure. First time he looked in the mirror and saw an old man staring back at him, absolutely. First hip replacement? Maybe, if that old hockey injury kept acting up.

But the lurching feeling in his gut was definitely not what he expected to feel for the first time now. That odd rush was something he should have experienced back in high school. Toward some sixteen-year-old girl who'd kissed him under the bleachers and then broken his heart by going to the prom with his best friend.

It wasn't lust. He knew lust. This was different.

"What's the matter?"

Nate put the bag down between them and rubbed his eyes, forcing a smile. "Not a damn thing."

She studied him and then crossed her feet and tilted her face up to the sun. "So what's in the bag."

Maybe there was a more reasonable explanation, he thought. Maybe some of those fritters he'd had for breakfast had been underdone. Or he was coming down with something. Or the height really was getting to him.

He craned his neck around, staring down at the lake and the expansive, yawning view. When his stomach heaved with alarm, he was reassured.

"I'm trying out a new recipe. Here—" he held out a piece of chicken "—ginger, garlic, herbs. Pretty simple stuff, but I like it."

She brushed off her hands, took a bite out of the leg, and chewed thoughtfully. He liked feeding her, liked knowing that something he'd made was passing over her tongue and going down into her body.

"It's good."

He smiled. "I know."

She shook her head, but he caught a hint of smile. "You've got a monstrous ego, you know that?"

He took out a piece for himself. "Yeah. But I'd also never give you something that wasn't my best."

"Trying to impress the boss," she said, lightly.

No, the woman, he thought.

"Maybe." He polished off a thigh and a leg and then settled back against a rock. He looked over at her.

"This is really good." She reached into the bag for another piece. "Are you going to put it on the new menu?"

"I don't think so. I'm keeping the number of selections small and everything is French. Two chickens, two fish, two meats. Until we get more customers, I'm not even going to bother with a dessert list. They'll have to be satisfied with whatever I make."

"God, I really hope this season's strong."

"But you're thinking of selling, aren't you?"

Her head snapped around. "Good Lord, no. What makes you say that?"

"The Englishman. I could see his head working like an adding machine as he went through the kitchen."

She looked down at the drumstick in her hand. "He's just a tourist."

"Hardly. That was Karl Graves, the international hotelier. He owns a dozen or so luxury hotels around the world."

She seemed stunned, but recovered quickly. "Then he can't be interested in buying White Caps. We're small fries to him."

Nate wasn't about to mention that the mansion would make a perfect private house for someone like Graves.

"How much trouble are you in, Frankie?" There was a long pause. "You can tell me."

Her chin angled up. "But I don't have to."

"No. You can hold it all in until you explode. Which is a great coping mechanism, assuming the people around you can handle the shrapnel."

"You trying to play therapist?"

"Maybe. Mostly, I'm trying to be a friend."

Which was, mostly, the truth.

He also wanted to have her naked, in his bed, writhing under him, scratching at his back. As all kinds of hot visions shot through his head, he prayed he still had a good poker face and that she wasn't a mind reader. Because he was damn sure she'd bolt down the mountain at a dead run if she knew what he was imagining.

He was trying to play his cards right. Considering how she'd shut him down after their first kiss, he'd been careful to give her plenty of space, hoping that she would come around, come to him. Unfortunately, she gave him a wide berth during the day. And every morning he woke up having not been disturbed.

After a week of unrelenting, lusty yearning, he'd cracked. He couldn't stand staying away any longer. Which was why he'd asked her to go up the mountain with him. A little time alone...another chance to kiss her...

He rearranged his body on the rock, feeling his shorts get tight.

Trouble was, as much as he wanted to take things in a carnal direction, it was more important for them to talk right now. She'd been clearly thrown by the visit to the graveyard and he wished like hell he could help her. He knew there was no way she was going to open up about her parents. So business was a second-best alternative.

"Look, I promise to keep my mouth shut," he said, trying to get her to talk about her problems. "And you can fire me if I don't."

The corner of her lips twitched as she leaned forward and locked her arms around her knees. He wanted to pull her over against him and tuck her head into his shoulder. But given how stiff she was, she didn't look as if she'd accept anything of the sort, so he stayed where he was, hoping she'd give him a chance to say the right thing. He wanted to tell her she was doing the best she could. That she was giving it her all. That if the place failed, it wasn't for her lack of trying.

Because he'd do just about anything to take back that idiotic comment he'd made the night he'd first met her.

She cleared her throat. "We'll survive somehow. We always have. I'm scraping the bottom right now, but that's nothing unusual for the start of the season."

"Do you owe a lot on the place?"

"Too much." She shifted. "The yearly taxes are huge, the upkeep is ongoing, and business has been off. And we've got a big debt burden because the house had to go through my father's estate when he died."

"It wasn't left to your grandmother first?"

She shook her head. "Her father still hadn't forgiven her for marrying someone he considered beneath her so it went to my dad when he was twenty-two. He was the one who decided to turn it into a B & B a couple of years later. Back then, business was good. Not enough to make the family wealthy again, but certainly enough to keep us comfortable."

Frankie looked up at the sky.

"I keep hoping things will improve. And I have thought about selling, but not seriously. Always in the back of my mind I think, if I stop now, I'll cheat us out of the salvation that's coming any minute." She laughed awkwardly and flashed him her eyes. "But that's optimism for you. A rose-colored torture chamber."

He admired her grit. "What kind of assets are left?"

"You mean art and jewelry? Not much. Not enough. I sold off a set of sterling flatware and the last of my grandmother's rings to send my sister to college. Joy finished UVM in three years." The warm pride in her voice quickly faded. "Although I think that was because she knew money was tight and Grand-Em was having such difficulties."

"Where did you go to college?"

"Middlebury. I didn't graduate." There was no apology in her voice. "I'd had some good plans, but they didn't work out. Though I don't know how well I would have done in the real world, anyway."

"Real world? So what do you think you're living in here?"

She rolled her eyes at him. "Saranac Lake is hardly the big leagues. It's not New York City."

"Is that where you wanted to end up?"

There was a long pause. "That's where I thought I was going to end up."

"What happened?"

She stood up abruptly. "Let's go back. I have to get the dining room set up."

"Why? It's Tuesday. We're closed."

She seemed to stall out. "The plumber. The plumber's in my office. He'll need to be paid."

Nate told himself that pushing her was not the answer. Patience, on the other hand, might just get him where he wanted to go.

Yeah, and where was that exactly?

The idea that he'd made a destination out of her concerned him. Just like that pit in his stomach, which, in spite of the chicken he'd just eaten and the fact that he wasn't looking at the lake, was still with him.

Nate stared up at her. "I'm glad you talked to me."

"I don't know why I did." She started bouncing from foot to foot as if warming up for the trip down the mountain.

He stood, brushed off his shorts and grabbed the bag. He kept his voice causal. "We all need a friend at one time or another. You can pay me back in kind some-time."

He started for the trail and was surprised when she didn't follow. He looked over his shoulder to find her staring at him, a hard light in her eyes.

"I meant what I said, Nate. We aren't going to get close."

"So we'll just have sex. And I won't ask anymore prying questions." He smiled, even though getting the stiff-arm from her hurt.

"I'm serious. I don't want anything from you."

He narrowed his eyes, thinking about their kiss. "You sure about that?"

"Positive."

And just what was so damn wrong with him, he wondered grimly.

She brushed a piece of hair out of her face. "I don't want you as a lover or a friend."

"Oh, that's right. Because you've got so many of both."

"Just leave me alone."

Two long strides had him next to her. He was of a mind to point out that relying on others wasn't a capi-tal crime, but she stepped back in alarm, as if he might force himself on her. It was like getting slapped. That she thought he was that kind of man.

Nate lifted his arms, holding his hands away from her.

"You want to be left alone? You got it, lady," he growled. "Just give me a five-minute head start so we don't have to walk down together."

He turned and headed for the footpath, not at all sur-prised when she did nothing to stop him.

Ah, hell. Instead of fighting for her, he should let her go. She wasn't interested in a casual lay and that was all he could offer her because he didn't do relationships. As for the friends bit? What a load of horse manure that was. As far as he was concerned, they could be lovers or nothing.

Nate dragged a hand through his hair, not real impressed with the way he was thinking about the situation. Lovers or nothing? God, he sounded like such a guy.

But damn it, if he was honest with himself, her rejection hurt. And he wanted to lash out at something.

So maybe he should go for a run when he got back to the house.

Yeah, like to Kentucky and back.

Several days later, Frankie surveyed the dining room from the mahogany hostess stand at the door. It was Friday at eight o'clock and they had fifteen out of twenty tables filled. The surging volleys of talk cut through the classical music playing from the stereo.

Word about Nate had gotten out around town and the locals were coming to sample the new chef's food. People she hadn't seen except for when she was doing errands in the square were coming back to eat at White Caps. As she looked at all the filled seats, she had to remind herself not to get excited, not to find the lifeline she was looking for in what might only be a one-time tryout for the patrons, not a trend.

But there were plenty of new things for them to try. Nate had completely reinvigorated the menu. It was all nouvelle cuisine now and the words were in French with English translations he'd written out for her. She'd typed the text up on the computer, bought some heavy, creamy paper usually used for resumes and printed out new inserts for the leather bound menu folios they'd been using for twenty years.

As a couple came through the door, Frankie smiled, unsheathed two menus, and led the way across the room. Generally, Joy played hostess because she was better at it. Looked better, too. But Grand-Em wasn't doing well tonight so Frankie was picking up the slack as well as busing tables. The two college girls she'd hired as waitresses were working out well, but if business kept up, they might need even more help.

Although this time she'd try and hire a guy. Because watching Rachel and Theresa drool over Nate was wearing thin and the girls had only been around for a week. God, the constant giggling and jiggling was driving Frankie nuts.

Although she was not jealous. Or being possessive. Really.

She was on the way back to the hostess stand when a woman reached out and waxed poetic about the chicken she was eating. As the guest insisted her compliments be sent along to the chef, Frankie smiled, nodded and thought that short of slipping Nate a note, she wasn't sure how she was going to do that.

Nate had given her just what she'd asked for. He hadn't looked at her or spoken more than three words to her since he'd left her on the mountain. His inventory reports were on her desk in the morning and he was always busy at the stove whenever she came through the kitchen. When she'd given him his paycheck and tried to thank him for all his hard work, he'd nodded curtly and walked out on her.

Typhoid Mary had gotten more attention from a man.

This was really not what she wanted. They needed to have a good professional relationship and the silent treatment was making work uncomfortable. She also couldn't really understand the total cold shoulder and wondered if maybe she'd hurt his feelings a little. But that seemed like a really arrogant assumption. Especially considering he had a fan club of nubile twenty-year-olds.

At the end of the night, she went back to her office and added up the business they'd done. Thirty-five meals, plus drinks, plus tips. Over twenty-five hundred dollars. More than they'd brought in over a single night in a long time.

All because of Nate.

She looked up from the receipts. If this continued, she was going to catch up with the mortgage just fine by the end of October. And the timing was great. The meeting with Mike at the bank had been tense, even though he'd assured her that he wasn't going to fore-close. She figured she'd call him in the morning, share a little good news and take some pressure off of him.

Joy stepped into the doorway, looking worn out. "Grand-Em's finally asleep."

Frankie could imagine how her sister had spent the night. Distraction was the only thing that worked when the delusions got really strong and it was hard to come up with games and tricks for hours straight. Grand-Em might be losing her grasp on reality, but her mind was as quick as it always had been.

"How are you holding up?"

"I'm pooped. She's still obsessed about finding her ring. She keeps insisting it's in the wall in her old bed-room. We also had more noise than usual downstairs so I think that kept her going, too. We sounded busy."

"We were."

"Nate's really wonderful, isn't he? We're so lucky he came by. He's made such a difference."

Frankie nodded and glanced down at the evidence.

Her sister frowned. "You don't seem to like him much."

"He's a good chef." She kept her eyes fixed on the paper.

"You really think so?"

"Of course."

"Have you told him?"

Frankie looked up. "Sorry?"

"Nate. In case you haven't noticed, he doesn't look real happy. Have you told him how much you appreciate his work?"

"I've tried. But I'll give it another shot."

"Good. I'm heading up." Joy lifted her hand and disappeared.

Frankie shuffled papers for a few minutes and then decided to grab the bull by the horns and go talk to him.

But the kitchen was empty. Everything was in its place, the dishwasher was churning over a load, the stainless steel counters were wiped clean.

She headed upstairs. His door was open, his light was off, his bed empty.

Where was he?

Frankie went back down to the kitchen. The house was quiet, the guests having gone to bed early to sleep off their sunburns and swim-sore muscles. She went outside through the back door, hoping to find him on one of the porches.

The night was a tender one, the breeze off the lake gentle, the moon glowing overhead. But he wasn't in any of the wicker chairs and she was about to turn around when she saw him, twenty yards away, standing on the dock. He had his hands on his hips and was looking down into the water. She started across the lawn.

And stopped when he took off his shirt. He tossed it behind him carelessly. Then shed his pants, too. There were no boxers or briefs for him to remove.

Good God, his backside was fantastic.

She put her hand over her mouth, thinking she really shouldn't wonder what the front of him looked like. But, oh, man, she could just imagine.

What a beautiful, powerful, naked man. He was like something out of a fantasy, drenched in moonlight, the lake sparkling around him.

Nate glanced over his shoulder.

And caught her red-handed. Her heart rate spiked even more, if that was possible, and she wondered how she was going to explain herself. *Yeah, see, I was just out for a little stroll and, ah, damn, you're built like a Greek statue, did you know that?*

But he showed no interest in her at all. Just turned back around and dove into the lake with a clean slice.

Frankie frowned, and as tempting as it was to race back to the house, she decided to be a grown-up. She went down to the dock, as if seeing a man who looked as good as he did in his birthday suit happened to her every night.

He stroked out some distance and then rolled over on his back. If he was surprised that she'd taken a seat on the dock, he didn't show it.

"Something wrong?" he drawled. As if that would be the only reason she'd seek him out.

Nothing's wrong, she thought. Other than the fact that the image of his butt was now tattooed onto the backs of her eyelids. Every time she blinked, she kept seeing that tight—

"In a manner of speaking," she said huskily.

Yup, tonight was going to be such fun. Laying in the dark. Seeing his bare ass on her ceiling.

"Let's hear it then." He swam to the dock and hefted his upper body out of the water. His forearms supported his weight while the bottom half of him stayed in the lake.

This she could deal with. All she had to do was forget he didn't have a bathing suit on. It wasn't like she could see anything.

Although, jeez, his shoulders were magnificent, the muscles straining under his skin. His hair was slicked back from his face, making his eyes seem fierce and his jaw especially hard. Or maybe that was all because of his mood.

She cleared her throat. "I want to thank you for all your hard work. I can't believe how business has picked up."

"You're welcome."

There was a long silence. She glanced down at her hands. "And I want to apologize for how defensive I got up on the mountain. Even though we have to keep things professional, you really were just trying to be nice and I basically bit your head off."

"No problem." His tone was bored.

"I should have handled that better."

"Forget it. I have."

He dropped back into the water, pushed off the dock and floated backwards.

Now why did that have to sting, she thought.

"Yeah. Well." She pulled the scrunchie out of her hair and played with it.

"There anything else you have to say?"

"Ah, no."

"Then you better head up to the house. I'm about to get out of this water and I can't imagine you're going to want to be sitting there when I do."

She closed her eyes, picturing him emerging from the lake, water droplets clinging to his skin. He would come over to her and urge her down onto the dock, getting her clothes wet as he laid on top of her and kissed her—

"Good night, Frankie," he muttered.

She nodded, stood up and walked back to the house. Looking at the sky, she thought the night didn't feel the same. She wrapped her arms around herself. It wasn't quite so warm anymore.

Chapter Nine

When Nate went down to the kitchen at five o'clock the next morning, he was thinking about whipping up some mousseline sauce. He wanted to cook something tricky. He wanted to get caught up in deftly manipulating temperature, in coaxing egg yolks and butter and flour into a sublime accompaniment for veal.

Because in the last couple of days, he'd lost his sense of humor, his ability to sleep through the night, and any semblance of equilibrium.

Damn it, but he couldn't get that woman out of his head. He vacillated between wanting to yell at her, needing to beg, or thanking the Lord she had the sense to put a wall up between them. And her little visit last night when he'd been skinny-dipping had been the kicker.

Because water, when running over naked skin, felt a

lot like a woman's hands. Especially when the female you wanted was sitting on the dock in front of you.

As if he needed the flipping reminder that he was desperate for her. Even though she was resolute about keeping them apart, he just couldn't seem to let the attraction go. First of all, he saw her every day. And even though he pretended to be busy as hell whenever she passed through the kitchen, he always watched her out of the corner of his eye. Talk about a recipe for disaster. He'd almost cut off his pinkie last night with a butcher's knife. And making things worse, he was sharing a bathroom with her. So every time he went in to take a shower, he thought about her naked, soaping herself down with the same bar he was using on his own body.

Man, if he didn't snap out of it, he was going to cut something off that wouldn't grow back. And have to start bathing in the lake.

At least this wouldn't last forever, he thought, opening the walk-in. Spike was on his way back to New York to scout out another place. And whether it was the right one or not, Labor Day would eventually come.

As Nate stepped into the cool, his eye caught a tomato that had rolled into a far corner. When he picked it up, the skin broke and the insides oozed all over his hand. The thing was rotted out, had probably been there for weeks.

This was totally unacceptable. One thing CIA had drilled into him was the importance of a clean kitchen. He should have done a complete scrub on the damn thing the moment he took over, but he'd been busy dealing with other stuff.

Like his fixation on his boss.

It took him close to a half hour to empty the walk-in, and when he was done, the kitchen looked like a farmer's market. There were squash and zucchini sticking out of pasta pots, corn still in the husks lined up on the table, heads of cauliflower and broccoli seated in chairs. He took the crates and steel bins the vegetables had been sitting in and hit them with the industrial spray nozzle that hung on the side of the dishwasher. Inside the walk-in, he disinfected the floor and every shelf with a bleach and lemon solution.

Then he started to tackle the kitchen floor. He was down on his hands and knees, his head wedged between the stove and the counter, his arm pushed back as far as he could force it, when he heard Joy's voice.

"My God, what brought this on?"

Your sister and her asinine need to be left alone, he thought.

Nate straightened, dragging the cloth towards him on the tile. It was black with filth when he picked it up. "I'm surprised you made it through state inspection. This place needs to be hosed down."

Joy leaned a hip against the island. "Can I help?"

"Go out and say good morning to Stu." He nodded at the window, to the truck that had just pulled up. "He's way early."

Stu and Joy did their best to arrange the new produce on what remained of the counter space and then Joy went into the office to get a check, while Nate told the man what they'd need for the next delivery. Stu had just taken off when frantic footsteps were heard from overhead.

"Frankie must be up," Joy said, glancing to the ceiling.

Nate was swallowing a curse when a man in a bath-robe burst into the kitchen from the dining room.

"There is an old woman in our bedroom! And she's cornered my wife!"

"Oh, no, Grand-Em." Joy rushed over. "I'm so sorry. She's utterly harmless."

"She has a hammer!"

Nate started to run after them, but Joy stopped him. "It's better if I deal with it."

She was so sure of herself that he deferred to her command, overriding his instinct to help by getting back on his knees and rinsing out the rag. He was reaching behind the stove again when he heard a hiss that brought his head up. Frankie stood at the foot of the stairs, staring in disbelief at the chaos. Her hair was damp and she'd frozen in the process of tying it back.

"Tell me the walk-in didn't die," she said.

"Walk-in's fine."

"Did Stu come already?"

"Just left."

"My God, what have you done?" He frowned as she marched up to the vegetables that were choking the is-land. The helpless, panicked look on her face quickly changed into anger. "Was Stu paid?"

"Of course."

"With what?" she demanded.

Their eyes clashed as he got off the floor. "Rubles."

"You think this is funny?"

"Not in the slightest."

She jabbed a finger at him. "I thought you and I agreed you would submit orders through me."

"And. I. Did," he said through gritted teeth, not ap-preciating her tone.

"So what's all this? You don't have the authority to place orders or accept deliveries. You're way out of line."

"Excuse me?" He put his palms flat on the stainless steel and leaned over a thicket of romaine.

"What the hell do you think we're going to do with all this food? The walk-in is full already."

Trying not to explode, Nate looked down at the floor that he'd been prepared to spend the next hour scrubbing.

"Screw this," he muttered and went for the door. He wasn't sure where he was headed. As long as it was away from her, he didn't care if he ended up walking to Canada.

"Where are you going?"

"I can't deal with you right now."

"But what about this mess?"

He threw the back door open. "Clean it up yourself or let it rot. I don't give a damn."

Frankie's heart was going like a snare drum as Nate walked out on her. She looked around the kitchen, taking in a fortune in produce that was gradually wilting, and almost burst into tears. She could only imagine how much it had all cost and confronting the mammoth order was like being sucker punched.

This was precisely what she'd wanted to avoid. Some hotshot chef thinking he was the second coming and overdoing it. Still, she was surprised. Somehow she'd thought Nate understood the kind of financial constraints they were operating under. Especially after what she'd told him on the mountain.

Maybe he was getting back at her. Although that didn't seem like him.

Yeah, but just how well did she know the man?

Frankie picked up a sack of potatoes and muscled it over to the walk-in. Cracking the handle and propping the heavy door open with her hip, she tugged the weight inside and looked up. Her breath left in a rush.

The walk-in was spotless. And empty as the day it'd been installed.

She looked over her shoulder. There was a bucket of suds and some rags on the floor behind the island. The milk crates that held the lettuce and the broccoli as well as the six- and eight-quart stainless steel drop-ins that corralled the tomatoes, mushrooms and celery were almost dry next to the dishwasher.

"Oh…hell." She put her hand on her forehead.

Twenty minutes later she had all the vegetables back in the cold and a pretty good idea of what she was going to say to him.

She headed for the barn and wasn't surprised she'd guessed right. Nate's lower body was sticking out from underneath the Saab, and given the urgent clanking noises, it sounded like he was being rough with his hands. No doubt he wished the car was in working order so he could put it to good use.

"Nate?"

The banging stopped. When he didn't say anything, she hitched up her pants and put down her pride.

"I'm sorry."

The noises started up again, softer now.

"Nate, I totally jumped to the wrong conclusion. I should have known you wouldn't do something so irresponsible." She waited for a response. When none came, she cleared her throat. "Anyway, I just wanted you to know how badly I feel."

Man, she was getting damn handy with the apologies. Two in less than twenty-four hours. The only problem was, they didn't seem to work.

She turned away.

"You know what pisses me off the most?" he said.

Frankie wheeled around as he wriggled his body out and sat up, dangling his hands on his knees. His fingers were black with grime, and when he scratched his forehead, he left a smudge over his eyebrow.

"You didn't even give me a chance to explain."

She closed her eyes. "I know. I was wrong. I overslept, came downstairs and saw all that food and…I totally panicked. I've been running this place on a shoestring for so long. I figured you'd forgotten you weren't down in the city."

"Trust me. I know where I am." And the tone of his voice suggested he'd rather be in New York.

She didn't blame him. God, he must miss the excitement, the pace. He'd been here…more than two weeks, she thought. And even though she'd promised him he wouldn't have much to do, he'd been busy in the kitchen as well as working on the house.

"Why don't you take Tuesday night off?" she suggested. "I can even loan you my car if you want to go into town."

"You trying to make it up to me?"

"I am." She offered him a small smile. "And I want you to know that I really do appreciate the work you've done. That walk-in is positively sparkling and your cooking is wonderful. You've done so much."

He got to his feet and stared down at her. Didn't seem to be too open to anything she was saying.

"I—ah, I hope that you don't leave."

"Because business is up, right?"

She nodded and thought he looked annoyed.

"Tell you what." He crossed his arms over his chest. "I'll take the night off if you do, too. We'll go into town together."

He shot her a sardonic smile as she started backpedaling. "Oh, I don't—"

"Think about it in terms of business."

She cocked an eyebrow.

"Six weeks is a hell of a long time. You and I need to figure out how to work together or one of us isn't going to be standing at the end of the summer."

"Why don't we just talk about it now?"

"Because I'm still pissed at you." She hesitated and he picked up an Allen wrench. "You can take my offer or not. But if you don't, I'm not going to be here tomorrow morning."

"That's one hell of an ultimatum."

"And I don't play games. So what's it going to be?"

Frankie looked deeply into his eyes. "Is seven good for you?"

"Perfect," he muttered as he got down on the floor and inched back under the car.

On Tuesday night, Nate got out of the shower and toweled off, thinking that he'd never before had to coerce a woman into having dinner with him. Threatening to quit a job was a new addition to his dating repertoire and he couldn't say he was happy with the fresh approach.

Damn that woman. She'd pushed him away, refused his friendship and then insulted him. Not once, but twice. And he still wanted her. What the hell was it going to take to turn him off? Having her knock him upside the head with a two-by-four? He was a man who thrived on challenges, but this was ridiculous.

And no matter how many times he reminded himself that they weren't going on a date, he supposed on some deep level he was hoping she'd be dazzled by him and come around. But no doubt that wouldn't happen unless something hit *her* on the head.

So this was desperation. God, what a drag.

Nate left his room wearing clean everything. Socks and boxers were just out of the wash. Khakis and the faded polo shirt were fresh from the duffel. He looked as presentable as he ever got.

He tried to remember the last time he'd been in a suit. Years, probably. Ties irritated the hell out of him and the only jackets he could stand were the top half of chef's whites. And the *GQ* rebellion stuff wasn't a new trend. He and his mother had always fought over his wardrobe and she'd given up only when he'd moved away from home and she didn't see him anymore.

So it felt a little odd for him to be wondering what Frankie would think if he were a sharp dresser.

She was waiting for him in the kitchen and he clamped his mouth shut so he didn't blurt out how good she looked. She was wearing a long, loose skirt and she'd left her hair down. Her blouse was just tight enough so that the curve of her breasts showed.

"You ready?" he asked.

She nodded as she picked up her bag and her keys. "George? We're going."

The man came in from the pantry. "Where you guys headed?"

"Nowhere special and we'll be home soon."

Nate wanted to shake his head. Yup, this was a woman looking forward to being alone with him, all right. Man, she kept at it and his ego was going to be the size of a cherry tomato at the end of the summer.

"Joy's going to heat up some dinner for you all," she said to George.

"I can do that. She's busy with Grand-Em."

Frankie smiled at the man. "You're thoughtful. We'll see you later."

"So where are we going?" Nate asked as they stepped out the back door and walked over to the Honda. The night was coming on and the temperature cooling.

"The Silver Dollar Diner. The only other choices are tourist joints that are more bar than restaurant. They're noisy, full of college kids out for the summer. It would be hard to talk business in them."

Nate smiled grimly as she opened her own door.

Right. Business. This was all about business.

He'd known carpenter ants who were less single-minded than she was.

In less than ten minutes, they were parked next to an old railroad dining car that had been put up on a foundation. Inside, there was a long, Formica counter with stools bolted to the floor and a soda fountain set up behind it. Red Naugahyde booths took up the other side of the car and stretched out into a back room that had been added on. The place had a well-used air and he had a feeling that the 1950s decor wasn't cultivated, it was authentic. The thing had probably been at the side of the road since sock hops and ducktails were in.

People looked them over and waved at Frankie. She was careful to introduce him as her new chef to every single person they talked to, setting the boundaries like a brick layer. He wasn't sure whether the message was for his benefit or the townspeople's—probably both. When they finally sat down at a booth way in the rear of the addition, he wasn't surprised when she put her back to the door.

Cherry tomato? His ego was going to fit on a pinhead with room to spare.

Before the waitress even filled their water glasses, Frankie said, "So. What do you think we should do?"

"Order dinner. Eat." Go dancing, he thought, eyeing the way her collarbones looked framed by the wide neckline of her shirt.

This is not a date, he reminded himself.

Yeah, says who, his libido shot back.

Nate rubbed his eyes. Oh, goody. He could kiss mental health goodbye now, too.

Frankie accepted a laminated menu with a smile. "I mean about us working together."

He flipped open his menu and was delighted to see pictures of the entrées. And the food was right out of the *Saturday Evening Post*. Meat loaf. Chicken potpie. Turkey blue plate special that came with mashed potatoes and wax beans. As if it could possibly have included anything else?

He felt her eyes on him and liked it, so he leisurely perused the selections.

"What are you going to have?" he asked.

"A nervous breakdown," she muttered and opened her menu.

So we'll tell the waitress to make that a double, he thought.

"I should never have agreed to this." Her eyes were

scanning up and down and he doubted she was seeing anything.

"Now why's that?" he drawled. And when she was finished, he could share his own list of regrets. Starting with the fact that he was getting turned on just by watching her lovely fingers flip the menu pages over.

"This just feels all wrong. And so does being around you in the kitchen. I can't decide whether you're ignoring me because you're busy or because you're still mad. And I tell myself I shouldn't care, but I do." She pulled the shirt back so its neckline was higher. Pity. "And if you are angry, I don't really blame you, but I can't think of much more I can do in terms of apologizing."

Unfortunately, he could think of quite a number of things. Most of which involved his mouth and unfettered access to her body.

Why don't you lean forward and put your hand on her knee, his libido suggested. You could inch that skirt up until you—

Shut up. Damn, his sex drive—

"Excuse me?"

Nate realized he'd spoken aloud. God, he hoped like hell he'd stopped at the *shut up* part. "Nothing. I, ah—"

The waitress came back. Thank God.

"We'd like a bottle of wine," he said. As well as a cold pack for his erection.

"White or red?" the woman asked, whipping out her pad.

"Frankie?"

"Red's fine. No, white. Wait, red." She put her hand on her forehead. "Oh, I don't know."

"We'll take one of each." He smiled at the waitress and ordered the meat loaf.

"That's overkill," Frankie said.

"Then pick one. And what would you like to eat?"

"I'll have the meat loaf, too. So red would be fine."

Out of the corner of his eye, he saw the door to the diner open and a tall man with two blond children come in. The three of them took seats at the counter. The youngest, a girl of about four, needed help from her father to get on the stool.

A sturdy shot of pain whipped through Nate's chest and he had to take a quick drink of water.

As he looked away from the kids, he hoped the ache would fade quickly. God, that yearning, that regret, was it *ever* going to go stop? Every child he saw triggered the sting. Especially the little girls.

And children were *everywhere*. He couldn't seem to get away from them, even at White Caps. Twice this week he'd had them invade his territory, coming into the kitchen looking for a snack or just out of curiosity.

"Nate?"

"Huh?"

"About us."

Good. Distraction was good.

He leaned back as the waitress put a bottle of wine and a basket of rolls on the table. He offered both to Frankie, who only let him fill her glass.

"Honest truth?" he said. "I'm not good at dealing with bosses to begin with and you've got some serious control issues. So I think we'll end up killing each other."

"But I apologized."

"And I appreciated it. Except that doesn't change much, does it?"

Her eyes flashed up to his. "So why are we here tonight?"

Because evidently he had a penchant for self-torture. God, could she look better?

Salads were put down in front of them. He watched her pick up her fork and carefully shuffle the radish shavings off to the side.

"Tell me, what's your problem with bosses?" she asked.

He started eating. "Same as everyone's. I don't like to be told what to do."

"Even if they're right?"

"But if they're right, I already know it and don't need to be told. And if they're wrong, they're wasting my time."

"That's pretty arrogant."

"You've already noted my healthy ego, so this can't be a surprise."

He caught her mouth twitching as if she were fighting a smile. "But when I spoke with Henri, he told me he was willing to give you everything to stay in his kitchen. You would have had control. Why did you leave?"

"If I'd taken over for him, I'd have always been in his shadow. He's a famous chef and that's a famous restaurant so I'd never make a name for myself. I'd just be keeping his alive after he retired."

"Do you want to be famous?"

"I want to be respected. And I want something that is *mine.* That's why I need to buy my own place in the city."

"Is New York your first choice?"

"Yeah."

She pushed her salad away and looked out the small window. She hadn't eaten much.

From the corner of his eye, he watched as the man

with the two kids got up and held his hand out to his younger daughter. She slid off the seat and together they started to make their way to the unisex bathroom which was in the far corner. The door squeaked a little when the man opened it and they went inside together.

Nate rubbed the throbbing spot in the middle of his chest. The sight of the little girl's hand in her daddy's sure grip made him sick to his stomach. He gulped some more water.

"What's wrong?" she asked.

"Nothing."

Chapter Ten

The waitress came by again, putting a bottle of ketchup between them and saying that their dinners would be out in a few minutes. As she walked off, Nate heard the bathroom door open and then the father and daughter were standing at their table.

"Frankie?"

Her head snapped around, her face settling into a frozen smile. "David."

The man smiled. "You're looking well."

"You, too. And this must be Nanette?"

"No," the little girl piped up. "That's my sister. I'm Sophie."

"And there's another one on the way," the man said with an awkward shrug, as if apologizing for his wife's fecundity.

Nate avoided looking at the little girl and narrowed

his eyes on the guy. He was tall, in good shape. Expensive watch and shoes. Had that genteel air of old money about him.

"How is Madeline?" Frankie asked.

"Very well. Getting bigger everyday. But she still keeps up with all of her work. That woman chairs more boards than I have clients." The man cleared his throat. "But you—ah, you must be busy, too. With White Caps."

"Yes, very busy."

The man looked at Nate as if he were searching for a life raft. "Where are my manners? I'm David Weatherby."

Nate recognized the name immediately. The Weatherbys and the Walkers had crossed paths often. But the last thing he wanted was to play connect the social dots, so he shook the man's hand and kept his lineage to himself.

"I'm Nate. The new chef at White Caps."

"Oh." The man inclined his head towards Frankie. "How are things this season?"

"Fine."

"Daddy. I want to go sit down now," the child said.

"Yes, darling. Ah, if you'll excuse us? Frankie, it was good to see you."

"Same here, David." Frankie let out a long breath after they left. "May I have some more wine?"

Nate poured, watching her as he filled her glass. "Old friend?"

"Something like that." She drank. There was a silence. "You aren't going to pry?"

"Don't need to. It's pretty obvious."

"Oh, really." She lifted the glass to her lips again.

"The two of you were lovers, right? Nasty breakup followed. But it's a small town so you know you will run into each other. Both of you are determined to be pleasant when it happens—"

"He was my fiancé." When she emptied her glass, she refilled it herself.

Nate shifted in the booth. That was more than he'd expected. He measured the man again.

Those could have been her daughters, he thought. And she'd probably considered the same thing once or twice.

The waitress put two plates the size of river barges down in front of them, asked if either of them wanted fresh pepper, and left when they declined.

"Why did it end?"

Frankie stuck with her wine. "My old life was over when my parents died. And neither one of us could see David fitting into my new one."

Nate paused with his fork and knife over the meat loaf. "He left you?"

"I told him to leave because I knew he was going to." She pushed her food around. "I think I was just a declaration of independence from his family, anyway. He'd always done what his parents expected of him and he was just getting out of college when we got together. His parents were trying to force him to go into the Weatherby brokerage firm down on Wall Street even though he was interested in journalism. Eventually, he caved in, but he brought me home the very first weekend after he started working. I was totally outside the standard. No money, working girl, loonies for parents. His mother wasn't happy and the more she complained, the more he said he loved me."

She tried a bite of the meat loaf. "I wanted to believe in him. In us. I was twenty years old and I wanted to live out a big, bright future in the best city in the world with a handsome husband who was devoted to me. But then my parents died and we postponed the wedding. After a while, I started to see the cracks in our relationship. Part of him had no doubt been honestly in love with me, but he was also using me. And I do think he would have married me if things hadn't changed in my family. He just wasn't prepared to strap on the remnants of my parents' lives and raise a teenager. His relief when I gave him back the ring was astronomical."

She laughed awkwardly, as if she was surprised she'd said so much. "But at least he cured me of any Prince Charming complex I might have had. Rich men are a huge turnoff. Between waiting on them hand and foot at my day job, and everything that happened with David, I'm sticking to my own kind from now on."

"Not everyone who comes from money is evil," he pointed out.

"True. But I've already gracefully endured the shocked disapproval of one rich man's family. I can't see myself behaving that well again. Now, I'm too old to put up with that crap."

"I can understand that." He picked up his water glass. "Did you like the city?"

"New York? God, yes. I loved it and not just the glamorous parts. I liked the way those street vendors' carts smell. You know the ones. With the roasting nuts?"

He nodded.

"And when I walked down Fifth Avenue at night, I could see that the sidewalk had flecks of mica or quartz or something in it that sparkled under the street lamps.

I liked the rush of the taxis and the shouts of the drivers. The horns. I liked Times Square with all the people and the lights." She cut herself off abruptly, as if enjoying the memories was too much of a guilty pleasure.

"Do you get down much anymore?"

"No. Although I do fantasize sometimes of moving there still. Which is ridiculous."

"Why?"

"It's never going to happen."

"Why not?"

Her brows twitched and her mouth flattened into a thin line. "There's White Caps for one thing. And my family. Joy needs me."

"But she's in her mid-twenties now, right? She's an adult so you're free. What's holding you here?"

She waved her hand through the air, as if his challenge was smoke she could bat away. "Let's change the subject."

"Why?"

"Because you're my chef, not my psychiatrist." With that, she picked up the bottle of wine and seemed a little surprised when it was almost empty. She looked at his glass, which was full. "You didn't like the taste?"

He shrugged. "I'm not a big drinker. The stuff's good in sauces and to clear the palate. Otherwise I avoid alcohol."

She sat back, studied him. "Any particular reason?"

"My father was a drunk." Her brows lifted with compassion. "Yeah, the smell of mixed drinks, especially anything with scotch in it, reminds me of him so I can't stomach the hard stuff. Wine's part of my job so I have a professional relationship with it."

"Do you see your father at all?"

"He's been dead for almost five years."

She put her fork down. "I'm sorry."

"I'm still not sure if I am, to tell you the truth."

Frankie considered him thoughtfully. "And your mother?"

"A little of her goes a long way. Fortunately, my brother tows the mark on that one. He takes care of her, thank God."

"Is she ill?"

"Healthy as a horse. But she could never support herself." Not with the kind of money she burned through on a monthly basis.

Frankie pushed her food around. Her face was full of concentration, as if she was trying to frame a difficult question.

"Have you ever been married?" she asked abruptly.

"No."

She fiddled with her mashed potatoes. "You say that as if marriage is an ugly thing."

His chest was speared again and his eyes shot over to the children at the counter. He thought of Celia, the woman he'd almost made his wife because he'd gotten her pregnant. The woman who'd taken his child away from him by going to a clinic and terminating the pregnancy.

Their pregnancy.

"You need any dessert?" he asked, not interested in food anymore.

"Don't you want a family someday?"

"Nope." He'd already tried that and had gotten burned so badly he couldn't stand to be around kids anymore.

"Have you ever been in love?"

"I thought we weren't going to be friends," he said gruffly. "So what's with the personal questions?"

"I'm just curious. Most people want to get married eventually, settle down, have—"

"Not me." There was a pause as she seemed to digest the brush-off. "You want a doggie bag for all that?"

She looked down at her full plate.

"George would like this," she allowed.

He called the waitress over and managed to pay for dinner before Frankie could. When they stood up to go, she looked over at David and his daughters. Gave them a little wave on the way out the door.

Thanks to the surfacing of both his past and hers, the air was thick between them as they walked over to the Honda. Parked next to it was a massive, shiny Mercedes Benz.

"I should drive," he said.

She tossed him the keys and then eyed the luxury sedan. "David always did like a big car. Fortunately for him, he could afford them."

When they were on the road, she looked over at him. "I don't want to go home yet."

"Fine with me. Where to?"

"Let's just drive. I don't care where we end up."

Frankie rolled down the window. She hadn't eaten much and the wine was doing its job, making her body lethargic and her head fuzzy. Because she was looking for a diversion and also because she really wanted to know more, she was tempted to press Nate about his past. But he was right. There was no need for her to be asking questions about his love life.

Although she had to wonder about the bitterness in his voice when he'd spoken about marriage… Had some woman done a number on him? If so, she couldn't blame him for not wanting to go into his ex-files. David was a hot button for her, too.

She looked at Nate. "I hate running into him."

His eyebrows rose. "David?"

"Every time I see him, he's wearing the same hang-dog expression he had on the day I called off the engagement. It's like he knows he was a coward. And maybe I should get some perverse pleasure out of the fact that ten years later he still feels badly, but I don't. I see him and his children and that fancy car and I want to remind him that he has it all. What the hell is he moping about? He's enjoying the *big life* in the city while I'm stuck here scraping out a living." She expelled a breath, anger surging as she imagined confronting him. "So don't come up to me looking like you're mourning something you're no doubt tickled freakin' pink that I let you bow out of gracefully! And grow up while you're at it! Be a man!"

She let her head fall back against the seat rest. "Sorry. I guess he's not in this car, is he?"

Nate laughed softly. "Not unless he snuck in the trunk."

"Then again, maybe he heard me back at the diner." She took a deep breath. "Sorry I yelled."

"I'd tell you to do it some more but I know that would shut you up faster than a strip of duct tape over that mouth of yours. So I'm just going to keep driving and hope you don't come to your senses."

"Why?" she whispered. "Why are you being so nice to me?"

He frowned, his eyes narrowing on the road. "Because you deserve it."

She fought against a tide of foolish gratitude. "Even after what I said when you cleaned out the walk-in? Even after that day on the mountain?"

"Yeah. Even so. You can be a real pain in the ass, but I think that's because you've had to be strong for so long. I don't mind cutting you some slack."

Tears pricked at the corners of her eyes. "Well. How about that."

They drove along in silence for a while and then she said, "Take a left up here. There's a great view of the lake at the top of this mountain."

He downshifted and took them to the summit. There were a few other cars in a small parking lot, well-spaced. It didn't take a genius to figure out what was going on inside of them.

Nate pulled into a slot at the far end and turned off the ignition.

She looked across the seat at his profile. "Tell me more about your family."

"Don't have much to tell."

"Which means there's probably too much to talk about, right?"

He smiled, his teeth flashing white in the darkness. "No. It means exactly what I said. They're not part of my day-to-day life."

"Where did you grow up?"

"Outside of Boston."

She waited for him to continue. When he didn't, she asked, "What about your brother. What does he do for a living?"

"He's a business guy. He's also into public service."

"That's admirable."

"Yeah. I respect the hell out of him." Nate shifted in the driver's seat, turning so he was facing her with one arm draped over the steering wheel. "So about us working together. Some things have to change."

She let her head fall back against the rest again.

Maybe it was the wine, but she suddenly didn't want to talk anymore. What she wanted was for him to lean over and kiss her on the mouth. Hard.

"What are your terms?" she murmured. "And you might as well know you have me over a barrel. I have to come up with $150,000 by the end of October."

He whistled softly and rubbed his jaw. "Will you be able to cover the debt?"

"If we do six more weeks of good summer business, I think I can make it because the leaf peepers come in the early fall. But it's going to be really tight. Especially if you leave. I've already put some feelers out for someone to replace you, but everyone's committed through Labor Day."

She stretched her legs out, until her feet got squeezed under the glove compartment. She hated anyone having power over her, but she wasn't stupid. She really needed Nate to stay.

"So what do you want?" she asked, not bothering to hide the acrimony in her voice.

"First of all, tell the guests to keep their children out of my kitchen. Twice this past week, I've been at the stove and some kid's come running in, looking for something to eat. They stay out of my space, got it?"

There was some serious tension in his voice and she wondered what it was all about. She could fully understand the safety issue, but she sensed there was something more.

"You don't like kids, do you?"

"Second, if business continues to be strong for another week, I want to hire a line cook. Nothing fancy and we could probably just find one through the want ads. George has come a long way, but he needs supervision and I don't want him hurt."

Nice avoidance of the question, she thought. Though the tone in his voice answered it well enough.

The man didn't want a wife. Didn't want children.

No wonder he was so comfortable with casual sex. It was either that or the life of a monk. And given the strength of his sex drive, she couldn't imagine he'd spend a single moment considering a life of celibacy.

"I have one more demand." Nate drummed his fingers on the dashboard. "If I stay, I want to spend some time with you. Alone."

Her head whipped around so fast, she pulled a neck muscle. "What?"

Nate watched her jerk to attention. "I think you heard me."

In the silence that ensued, she stared at him as if he'd lost his mind. Hell, maybe he had.

But that just meant he was a crazy man with some serious leverage. She needed him. And he knew what he wanted in return. He'd tried the direct route with her and been shut down. He'd tried ignoring the attraction. Yeah, right, that had worked. So maybe he could strike a deal.

"I am not going to sleep with you to keep my house," she told him flat out.

Ouch. That wasn't what he meant.

"Damn, woman, you really know how to throw an insult, don't you," he muttered. "Do you have a piss poor opinion of all men or is it just me in particular?"

"Come on, what am I supposed to think? You remind me that we're not supposed to be friends and then want to spend time with me. What are we going to do? Play Scrabble?"

Well, jeez, he wasn't an animal, for God's sake.

Nate measured the curve of her lips.

He wasn't a *total* animal.

And the reason he'd brought up the friend's only rule was to get her off the subject of his past. It was just a conversational obstacle he'd put up.

"All I want to do is go out with you a couple of times. No big deal. I'm talking dinner. And a movie, maybe. I'm not asking you to do the horizontal foxtrot."

Although if there was even a shot of that—

"But I want to know what for."

"Doesn't matter. It's what I want. Or do we need to review the balance of power between us again? Who needs who more?"

Her eyes narrowed on his. "I don't like you very much right now."

"Duly noted. Now what's it going to be?"

She paused. Looked at her hands. Pushed down a cuticle. "How many times?"

"Every Tuesday night."

Frankie started to shake her head. "I just don't understand you. Why would you—"

He reached across the seats, took her into her arms, and put his mouth on hers.

God, her lips were soft.

And when she didn't fight him, Nate groaned and deepened the kiss, his tongue sliding up against hers. His body had gone from sitting quietly to straining against his clothes and the change happened in the blink of an eye.

But Frankie Moorehouse could do that to him.

When he finally pulled back so they could both get some air, his voice was hoarse. "*That* is why. And I'm not saying we have to have sex. But if I can't touch you, I'm going to lose my friggin' mind."

Her hand lifted up and he wondered if she was going to slap him. But then he felt her touch on the back of his neck and she drew him down to her lips again.

Oh, sweet heaven, he thought.

He complied with her demand in a hungry rush, capturing her in a kiss that went on and on. When he felt her push against his chest, he kept his disappointment to himself.

"Take me home, Nate," she said in a shaky voice.

Ah, hell. He'd done it again. Too far, too fast. He wasn't surprised that she'd pulled back, but frankly he didn't know where she found the strength.

He started the car while trying to remember how to drive and the trip to White Caps was silent and mercifully short. When they walked into the kitchen, Frankie headed directly for the stairs and he figured he'd let her go. He was in no hurry to be across the hall from her while she was undressing.

"Nate?"

He looked over his shoulder.

"Aren't you coming upstairs?" she said with one foot on the first step.

He shook his head. "I think it's better for us if I stay on the first floor for awhile."

Hell, maybe he should take up sleeping on the counter.

Frankie flushed. "Oh. Because that's not what I'm thinking."

Nate stopped breathing. Was she telling him what he was dying to hear?

"I, ah, I thought we'd go up together."

Without hesitating for a nanosecond, he bolted for the stairs, grabbing her hand and towing her along with him.

After she shut the door to her bedroom, he took her face in his hands and kissed her softly on the lips. He pulled back, thinking that he wanted to ask her why now, why tonight? But he kept his questions to himself because he had a feeling he wouldn't like the answers. She'd seen her ex-fiancé. With his children. She'd had a little more wine than usual. The change of heart made sense, but curiously, made him feel like hell. He would have preferred to be chosen, not used as a refuge or a distraction.

But he would take her anyway.

As if his doubts showed in his face, Frankie looked him straight in the eye. "You're the only man in this room tonight, Nate. This isn't about seeing David. I've been thinking about making love with you since the moment you walked through my back door. I'm just tired of fighting it, I really am."

Nate crushed her to him. He told himself to take it slowly, but he was so hungry that his hands were shaking as he stroked her back. He kissed her deep and long as he maneuvered her backward towards the bed and he almost shouted with joy as she grabbed the bottom of his shirt and yanked it free from his khakis. Desperate to be naked with her, he pulled back and whipped that polo off so fast, he was back at her mouth before the thing hit the floor.

And then they were on the bed. She was hot and restless under him as he slipped his hand under her skirt and dragged the fragile fabric up to her knees and then past her smooth thighs. Her hands were doing crazy things to his body, running over his back and slipping on to his ribs. He found the soft skin of her throat with his lips while parting her legs with his knee. As she cradled his hips with her own, he growled deep in his throat and concentrated on getting her naked.

However good he'd thought it would be between them, the reality blew the doors off his fantasies.

Frankie reached between them and fumbled with the fly of his pants as Nate undid the buttons down the front of her blouse. He lifted himself from her and kicked off the khakis while stripping off her shirt. She reached for the clasp of her bra, thinking she loved a man who could multitask.

"Oh, no, you don't," he said, stilling her hands. "I want to do that."

He kissed her again as he traced the lace edges of the bra with his fingertips, and his touch was gentle considering how frantic they both were. Her eyes met his. He was so hungry, she thought. The skin on his face was tight, as if he were in pain.

No man had ever looked at her like that. And she'd never imagined one would.

Cool air hit her breasts as he did away with the lace, and then the warmth of his palms was on her tender skin. She felt no modesty at all as his gaze fell upon her body. How could she? She saw herself reflected in his eyes, through the prism of his reverence and awe. In his arms, she was beautiful and she felt an absurd desire to thank him, but kissed him instead.

He nuzzled his way down her neck and over her collarbone, and then his lips brushed against the side of her breast. She arched up off the mattress as he took her nipple into his mouth, the warm, wet feel of his tongue making her cry out. He answered her with a groan of his own and reached underneath her, undoing the skirt. She pushed it off and entwined her legs with his, feeling the length of him pressing into her, all hard demand. God, he was deliciously heavy.

Her panties disappeared and his boxers were gone, and then it was skin on skin, mouths on mouths, hands seeking and finding pleasure.

"Condom," he mumbled against her neck. "We need a—oh God! Touch me again like that."

"Here?"

He let out a crazy moan. "Yeah. There."

Condom? Did she even have one?

"I don't—" She didn't finish because he kissed her, tongue deep in her mouth.

"Have one?" he said, when he pulled back to catch his breath.

"Yeah, I haven't done this in a while." If she had kept any around from her time with David, they would have turned to dust by now.

Nate leaped off her and jogged across the hall. "Let me see if I do."

The curse word that floated out of his room didn't inspire confidence.

He came back. "There a pharmacy around here?"

"Not open this late."

"Grocery store?"

She shook her head. "It's after ten."

"Damn."

He had a wild look on his face as he hesitated. Then he kicked the door closed and stalked over to the bed. She welcomed him with open arms.

"I'm totally into safe sex," she said, anticipation roaring through her. "But we don't have to—"

And then he suddenly stiffened against her. The lack of movement was a complete shock.

As she looked up, his eyes went dark, haunted. His face assumed a tortured expression, one that had nothing to do with the wanting.

What she'd been about to say was there were other ways for them to finish the evening off. Except now, all the heat appeared to have been sucked out of him. Out of the whole room.

"Nate?"

He seemed to shake himself from whatever had captured him.

"No buts," he said hoarsely. "About safe sex."

He kissed her again, but it wasn't the same. Something had taken him away.

"What's wrong?" she asked.

He rolled over on to his back, tucking her into his side. His hand stroked her shoulder, but it was a restless movement.

"Nate?"

His eyes were focused somewhere across the room.

"It's all right. Whatever it is," she said.

He finally looked at her. And she realized he was measuring her, although against what she wasn't sure.

"I'm really sorry," he said. "But I need to go."

Even though she'd been undressed for the last half

hour, she suddenly felt naked and pulled her top sheet around her body. "Okay."

He got off the bed, picked up his clothes and left.

Chapter Eleven

Nate dropped his shirt and pants on the floor and paced around his room naked. It was no big surprise that he'd come unglued.

Seeing that little girl with her daddy. Having Frankie suggest they could have sex without protection. And boom!…he was right back in the nightmare.

He sat down on the bed, put his head in his hands, and tried to breathe.

How old would his child have been now? Three. He or she would have been three.

If only Celia hadn't ended the pregnancy. If only he'd been the rich man she'd thought he was—

There was a soft knock on the door.

He pulled on some boxers. "Yeah."

He didn't look up as the hinges creaked. He knew who it was.

"I just wanted to make sure you're okay." Frankie's voice was warm, concerned.

He had to give her credit. There were few women who would handle the transition from hot and bothered to cold and deserted so well.

"Are you?" she whispered.

He wasn't going to lie to her so he kept his mouth shut. Because he wasn't okay. He hadn't been okay for a while although he'd gotten damn good at hiding it.

He felt the mattress dip down slightly as she sat next to him. She'd pulled on jeans and a long T-shirt.

"If you want to talk…"

"No." Because damn it, he was on the verge of tears. And there was no way he was going to cry in front of her. Going limp in her bed was enough of a cringer for one night.

"That's all right." She let out a small laugh. "I know all about keeping things inside as you've witnessed firsthand. So I'm good with silence."

He didn't answer her, but reached out and took her hand in his. Her skin was smooth, soft. He stroked his thumb over the pad of her palm.

"You know what?" she said.

"Hmm?"

"We keep this up, we might just get to be friends after all."

He looked over at her. She'd left her glasses back in her room. God, her eyes were lovely. So blue. A bottomless blue. He had the sudden impulse to get lost in her eyes, just let himself float away and trust that she would catch him. He opened his mouth.

Ah, hell. He couldn't do it. "I'm sorry, Frankie."

She reached up and brushed his hair back. "You've got nothing to be sorry for."

"That's where you're wrong."

"I don't care that we stopped. Well, I do. But I wouldn't want you to be with me if you had doubts."

Doubts? About being with her? He'd been so into her, he'd almost said to hell with the condom. And that was at the core of what killed him. That he'd been so tempted to throw out common sense just because he wanted her so badly.

Considering all he'd lost, you'd figure he would have learned something.

Self-hatred burned in his gut. With Celia, he'd been careless. With Frankie, he'd been close to losing control. Neither spoke well of him as a man.

"Will you let me stay with you awhile?" she asked. "Not to have sex or anything. Just to, you know, hold you."

"Yeah." He'd like that.

Nate leaned back against the pillow and she curled up at his side. Her breath drifted across his bare chest and her hand rested on his waist lightly. He crossed his feet at the ankles and closed his eyes. Her presence eased him.

"Now I know how hard it is," she said softly.

"What?"

"Wanting to help and not being able to."

He kissed her temple. "You are helping."

Frankie shifted, felt her thigh brush against warm, male skin and came awake instantly. She looked up into Nate's face. His beard had grown in overnight, darkening the thrust of his jaw. His hair was smudged this way and that. His eyes were open, lids low.

"Good morning," he said with a gravel voice.

"Hi."

The reserve hadn't left him. She still felt as though he was reining himself in. And as much as she still wanted to know what had happened, she wasn't about to ask him again. She hated when people did that to her.

"Guess it's time for breakfast." She shifted upright, swung her legs over the edge of the mattress and felt the cool pine boards under her feet. "It's going to be a busy week for us. We've got a whole family arriving today and…"

She chattered on, her voice sounding false to her own ears. But then that tended to be the end result when you were talking about one thing and thinking about another.

Did last night really happen? Was there actually a time they had been so close? Yeah, but only physically and that was the easiest way, wasn't it? Which was why people had one-night stands. No strings, but just enough intimacy to remind you that you could in fact relate to another human being.

"Frankie?"

She stopped mid-sentence.

"Last night ended because—" He rubbed his temples. "It doesn't have anything to do with you."

So he said.

"It's all right. Really. Probably for the best, too." She walked over to the door. "See you downstairs."

His eyes bored into hers. "Yeah. Downstairs."

But they didn't spend much time together that morning. He was busy at the stove, she was working in her office. But at least on the few occasions she passed through the kitchen, he looked up, met her eyes and nodded.

She was back at her desk, reviewing with satisfaction the way the dinner reservations were getting tight, when the phone rang.

"Is Nate there?" It was a deep male voice. Hint of an accent she couldn't quite place.

"Yes. Who may I ask is calling?" She blurted out the question on reflex, but she was really interested in the answer.

"Spike." The man's tone suggested impatience.

And considering the guy was named after a piece of hardware, she put two and two together and decided he probably wasn't into small talk.

"Hold on."

She called into the kitchen and Nate came right away, wiping his hands on the white apron he'd tied around his lean hips. She tried to keep her eyes from bouncing to his wide chest, and failed. His T-shirt was navy blue and had a worn logo on it, but all she could really see was the way his muscles had looked the night before, shifting under his skin as he'd held himself over her body while kissing her breasts.

Frankie got to her feet, wondering if he'd want privacy. Although even if he didn't, she needed a little air.

"Stay," he said as he picked up the phone. She sank back into her chair. "What's up? Where? Yeah, I know the place. When are you seeing it? How much they want for it?"

A couple of uh-uh's and another yeah followed. He hung up the phone, thanked her for getting him and left.

Frankie looked out at the lake, thinking that the reminder was a good one. Nate was a short timer at White Caps. As soon as Labor Day came, he was going back to the city to find his destiny as the next Bobby Flay.

And one day, a few years from now, she was going to crack open a magazine and read about the new, hit restaurant in New York City. There'd be a picture of him and she'd stare at it for a while, thinking what might have been if they'd made love.

But *might have been* was better than knowing exactly what she was missing. Right?

Oh, what a load of bull. She wanted him. Even if he was leaving. Even if it was going to hurt later.

"Frankie?" Nate was back, standing in the doorway of the office. "You got a second?"

She nodded and was surprised when he closed the door. Her body tensed, but she kept her expression as neutral as possible. She wondered if he was going to quit.

"I really appreciate you giving me some space." He dragged a hand through his hair.

She laughed stiffly. "You look like you're about to apologize for something."

"I am."

"Well, please don't." She didn't really want to hear about how he regretted getting what he'd asked for.

He grew quiet. Then took a deep breath.

"Okay. But I want you to know something. I'm dying to be with you. Tonight. Now. Right now." His eyes leveled on hers and they burned. "Would you consider giving me a second chance?"

Good Lord, was Santa Claus a fat man in a red suit? Of course, she would.

She got up from the chair because her body suddenly needed to move. Anticipation had replaced the dread she'd felt and the sweet rush was a hell of an improvement.

"Well, ah, it was pretty good," she said, trying not to come across as desperate. Although what an understatement that was.

Hell, with the door closed, she was tempted to sweep her computer off the desk just so they had a flat space to get busy on.

"It was a hell of a lot more than good for me," he said in a low, sexy tone.

Frankie looked at him, remembering the feel of him against her. "I want more of you," she said softly. "God help me. But I want more."

Nate came around the back of the desk and took her into his arms, pulling her against his body. With his hands on her hips, he drew her in close and she felt his arousal.

"So do I." His voice was deep, husky.

She put her hands against his chest and held him back. "But I don't expect you to stay once September gets here. This is just casual sex, okay?"

That was a lie, of course. She liked him. She really did, even though he was arrogant and demanding and she didn't know enough about him.

When the fall came, she was going to have a big clean-up job to take care of after he'd left, but she wasn't about to try and tie him down just so she felt better about sleeping with him. First of all, she was an adult, which meant she was fully capable of making a bad decision and having to live with the consequences. And second, he didn't owe her anything. Two and a half weeks ago they'd been total strangers and in another five or so, he would go back out into the world on his own.

"This is only causal sex," she repeated, as much for her own benefit as his.

Nate's eyes blinked once. "Whatever you say."

"So, are you going to the pharmacy or am I?"

That night the restaurant was a madhouse. People were actually waiting for tables and Nate was in his element. She'd never seen someone work so fast or so well.

At the end of the evening, even though she was wilted from all the work, she went to her office to add up the receipts. She had to go through them twice. They'd done five thousand dollars worth of business.

Was it possible that miracles really did happen?

When the phone rang, she picked up. "White Caps."

There was static and then, "Frankie?"

"Alex! Where are you?"

"Heading for home, believe it or not." More static. "—be there in about a week."

"A week?"

"—then we're heading back out—America's Cup training—"

"Alex?"

"—better go now. See you soon."

"I can't wait to see you!"

"Same h—" The connection broke.

She hung up the phone smiling.

"Who was that?"

She looked across the room. Nate was leaning against the doorjamb. He'd taken a shower and changed into cut-offs and his hair was wet, curling against his neck.

"Ah—my brother. He's coming for a visit." She got to her feet, feeling awkward.

Nate stared at her from under low lids, anticipation

coming off of him in waves, but she wasn't exactly sure how this was supposed to work between them. He answered the question by striding into the room and putting his hands on her waist.

"It's late. We should get to bed."

She slid her arms around his neck. "Funny, I was thinking the exact same thing."

Upstairs, she drew him into her bedroom and had a moment of trepidation as he undressed her. But the moment they fell onto her bed and his body was on hers, she stopped thinking. The sensations he roused as he suckled her breasts and swept his hand between her legs were all her brain could handle.

What a lover he was. Relentless, he pleasured her over and over again until she didn't think it was possible for her to climax one more time. Unfortunately, he refused to let her reciprocate. Every time she tried to reach for him, he stayed just out of range. He was generous to the point of frustration and she had a feeling he was making up for leaving the night before.

But his pleasure was hers.

"Why can't I touch you?" she moaned, trying to get to his erection.

His voice was rough in her ear. "Because I'm going to come the instant you do. God, I'm so hot for you."

And then he went back to work on her.

The only time he paused was to put the condom on.

His body was taut over hers as he came back to her. She reached for his hips to pull him down, but he resisted, resting his forehead on hers. His breath was ragged.

"Frankie, look at me. I want to see your eyes."

And then he sank into her body, filling her, stretching her. He was slow at first but then his thrusts gained power until she was climaxing again. As her body grabbed onto his, he went rigid, her name torn out of his throat.

As dawn came, Nate rolled over, pulling Frankie tightly against his body. He had to get up in a matter of minutes to start breakfast and wanted to savor the quiet moment.

She stirred in his arms. "Is it morning already?" Her voice was groggy as she rubbed her eyes.

"Unfortunately."

They'd made love twice more during the night and had fallen asleep only an hour before, but Nate felt like he could run a marathon.

He trailed his hand down the smooth plane of her stomach and then onto her thigh. "You know something?"

"What?"

Nate shut his mouth. He was going to say he could really get used to waking up next to her, but he thought about her casual-only limits.

Hell, his own casual-only limits.

As he kept his lip zipped, he thought, well, wasn't this was a new one. Usually women wanted him to talk to them and he had nothing to say. Or nothing they'd want to hear, to be more accurate.

But, God, after last night, he wanted to let loose with a whole stream of romantic drivel. She'd rocked his world and not just physically.

Frankie rolled over and looked up at him.

Man, he liked the color of her eyes.

"What?" she prompted.

"I gotta go." He dropped a kiss on her mouth and

then got out of bed quickly. He was pulling on his shorts when he caught her smile.

"You've got a beautiful body, you know that," she said, eyes going low.

He paused, glanced at the clock.

Breakfast could wait a little longer.

Chapter Twelve

Friday night, Joy looked up from the hostess stand and froze.

Gray Bennett towered over her, a smile on his sexy-as-hell face. He was dressed in white linen pants, a navy blue blazer and an open necked shirt. He was tanned, his hair was a little on the long side, and he looked better than any man had a right to.

"Hello, Joy."

She cleared her throat, not willing to take a gamble on her voice. "Good evening."

"How are you?"

She smiled, feeling a glow come over her like a heat lamp had been turned on above her head.

"Really well." Now that he was here.

"This place is packed." He glanced out across the tables. "I didn't know you had to make reservations."

She blurted immediately, "I can make an exception for you."

As well as making a fool out of myself, she thought. God, the eagerness in her voice made her want to wince.

He just smiled. "If you wouldn't mind?"

"Not at all." But she prayed he didn't have ten people with him. "How many?"

"Just my father and I."

Joy glanced to the door and saw Mr. Bennett talking to the mayor and his wife. Gray's father had had a stroke over the winter and was still recuperating, leaning heavily on a cane.

"I'll put you on the lake side. Come right this way."

She could feel him moving behind her and saw some of the other diners look up and whisper. Gray Bennett was something of a local celebrity, considering all of his political power and connections. It wasn't often that someone who hobnobbed with world leaders floated through town.

Although she knew the women would have stared if he'd been no more than a garage mechanic. That masculine air of his was an aphrodisiac like none other, capable of putting oysters in the shade.

"Would you like something to drink?" she asked as he sat down.

"A bourbon would be great."

"I'm sorry, we only have wine."

"Then a glass of something white is fine. And one for my father, too. Assuming he eventually ends his conversation with the mayor." He smiled up at her and opened his menu.

On the way to the kitchen, Joy checked her watch.

If everything went well, he'd be in their dining room for over an hour. Longer if he ordered dessert.

Sweet heaven, he was too handsome to look at.

As she poured two glasses of wine, she practiced the list of specials in her head, hoping she could come across smooth and in control. Like him.

She was heading for the double doors with a tray when Frankie called out, "Joy! We've got a problem."

Joy paused, looking through the round glass portals at Gray's table. He was helping his father sit in a chair.

"Joy!" Frankie's voice was sharp.

"What?"

"Grand-Em is back in the Lincoln Bedroom. Mr. Thorndyke just called. Can you go calm her down and get her into her own room?"

Joy squeezed her eyes shut. Not tonight. Not with Gray here.

"Pickup!" Nate called out.

"Joy?" Frankie said, coming over urgently and taking the tray from her hands. "I'll take these drinks out. Where to?"

"Table twelve," she replied.

Frankie shot over to Nate, put the two entrées he'd just plated on the tray next to the glasses and pirouetted out into the dining room.

A moment later Joy followed, on her way to the Lincoln Bedroom. As she passed by Gray's table, she heard Frankie telling him and his father about the specials.

She was out in the hallway before she had to look back. Gray was laughing at something Frankie had said, a big, wide smile on his face, his eyes creasing at the corners.

And then suddenly, he looked at her. He actually looked right through the crowded room, directly at her.

His smile lost some of its breadth and those stunning, shrewd eyes narrowed on her face. Joy stopped breathing.

As far as she was concerned, the whole world stopped moving.

But then Frankie looked over with a frown, as if she'd caught Gray's change in mood and was curious what the cause was.

Joy hurried away.

Holy Moses, what was that, she thought.

She took the stairs two at a time even though her legs were about as stable as her heartbeat.

Maybe he'd caught her staring and all her stupid fantasies had shown on her face.

Oh, God. The idea that he knew about her silly infatuation was enough to make her nauseous. Sure, in her daydreams he greeted the news flash with happiness. But in real life, she couldn't believe a man like him would feel anything other than pity for her.

When she got up to the landing, she saw the Thorndykes in the doorway of their room, looking worried.

"I'm so sorry about this," she said, stepping past them.

Her grandmother was on the floor, poking at the wall with a screwdriver.

Joy rushed over. "Grand-Em, is there something I can help with here?"

"You can get me into this wall. I must retrieve my ring."

"Okay. But why don't we do it some other time? We're disturbing these nice people."

Grand-Em hesitated, good breeding momentarily taming the dementia. "But the ring must be found."

"Of course it does. But wouldn't you agree we shouldn't inconvenience our guests?"

Grand-Em eyed the couple and accepted a hand up off the floor. "Yes, you are quite right."

Joy pocketed the screwdriver and shot apologetic glances at the Thorndykes as she led her grandmother down the hall to the door that opened to the staff quarters.

"I must find my ring."

Joy figured she'd give it one more shot. "But isn't it on your finger?"

Grand-Em looked down at her hand. "No, the one Arthur gave me."

"But Grand-Em, you were never—"

Joy's grandmother shot her an imperious stare. "I shall prove that he asked me to marry him. Come. I shall show you."

The next morning, Frankie sat at her desk and reread the letters her sister had given her the night before.

It looked as if Grand-Em wasn't delusional about Arthur Garrison.

There were four letters from him to their grandmother, dated between the fall of 1940 and summer of 1941. And sure enough, the last one demanded an answer to the proposal he'd made and the ring he'd offered to her that April. The words the man had used were flowery, over-the-top.

Artie was a real ladies man, Frankie thought.

The phone on her desk rang and she picked it up. "White Caps."

"Frankie? It's Mike Roy."

"Mike, how are you?"

"Fine." Funny, he didn't sound fine. "Listen, I've got some bad news."

Frankie let the letters fall to the desk as she gripped the receiver. "Hit me."

Literally, she thought.

"The bank is being acquired."

"Will you have to leave?" she asked, hoping she wouldn't lose him.

"I don't know. I hope not. But, ah, we need to settle up your account before the sale goes through. All business is being brought up-to-date."

"How much time?"

"End of August."

She put her head in her hands. "Okay."

It wasn't okay. Not by a long shot. But what else could she say?

"I'm sorry."

"No, it's not your fault. I'll get the money."

"Look, if you can't, I have an interested party."

"An interested—for the house?"

"Yes. It'll be better than putting it up for auction if you default. You'll get more money that way."

"The Englishman," she whispered. "The hotelier you brought here. Is he really a friend of yours?"

Mike cleared his throat. "I'm just trying to do you a favor."

"You knew about this all along, didn't you?"

"I wasn't sure the acquisition was going to go through. I'm giving you as much notice as I possibly can."

After they hung up, Frankie stared across her office, at the picture of her family.

The phone rang almost immediately.

Maybe he was calling back and telling her he'd made a mistake. Yeah, right.

"White Caps."

"May I please speak with Frances Moorehouse." The male voice was curt, authoritative.

"This is she."

The man cleared his throat. "Ma'am, I'm Commander Montgomery of the United States Coast Guard."

Frankie went stone-cold. "Alex?"

"It is with regret that I inform you that your brother, Alexander Moorehouse, is missing off the coast of Massachusetts. His vessel was found capsized in high seas in the eye of Hurricane Bethany. We have instigated a full search for both him and his sailing partner, Mr. Cutler. I'd like to give you my contact information, but be assured, I will call you with news."

Frankie could barely hold a pen and write she was shaking so badly. And as soon as she hung up, she bolted out of her office. Careening through the kitchen, she ran outdoors blindly. When she finally slowed down, she realized she was on the dock.

She looked out at the vast expanse of the lake.

And screamed at the water.

Nate saw Frankie come crashing through the kitchen and he immediately dropped what he was working on and went after her. She was running as if chased, and when she got to the end of the dock, she pitched her body forward and let out a roar of pain.

He reached out for her. "Frankie!"

She spun around, eyes wide with horror, tears streaking down her red, contorted face. "Alex is dead. My brother is gone."

Nate squeezed his eyes shut and crushed her against his chest.

As he wrapped his arms around her body, she fell

apart, sobs wracking her shoulders until he thought her spine would snap. The sounds coming out of her were like that of an animal.

When he glanced up and saw Joy slowly coming down the lawn, looking worried, he pulled away slightly.

"Your sister," he said softly in Frankie's ear.

Frankie pulled back, wiped her eyes with hands that trembled, and sniffled. He gave her the dish towel he carried in his back pocket while he worked.

"Frankie?" Joy's voice barely carried.

"I'll leave you two," Nate whispered.

Frankie gripped his hand. "No, stay."

"What's happened?" Joy asked.

"Alex—" Frankie's voice cracked. "Alex."

Joy's face collapsed, her mouth, her eyes, the bones in her cheeks sagging. And yet her voice was strong when she spoke. "Is he missing or dead?"

"Missing. But—"

"So there's a chance."

"His boat capsized. In a hurricane."

"And if anyone could survive that, it would be Alex." Joy lifted her chin. "I'm not mourning him until they find his body."

Joy turned around and headed back for the house. Her hands were wrapped around her slender body, her strawberry blond hair lifted by the wind.

Nate looked at Frankie. "She's strong."

"Stronger than I am right now." She glanced over her shoulder, her eyes grim as they leveled on the lake. "I can't bear to lose him, too. God, why the hell is water so hungry for my family?"

Nate put an arm around her. He wanted to tell her that

it would be okay and they would find her brother. But no one except the good Lord could know what the outcome was going to be. "You want to close the dining room tonight?"

Her chest expanded as she drew a deep breath. "No. We need the money."

Eventually, they went back to the house and Frankie stayed in her office. When the kitchen was closed down, Nate went to her. She was staring out the window, one hand on the top of the desk, right next to the phone.

"Did we do well tonight?" she asked dully.

"Yeah."

"Good." She finally looked at him. "I tried to talk to Joy, but she won't listen."

Nate went around the desk and knelt down in front of her, putting his hands on her knees. "You want to go upstairs?"

When she shook her head, he sat on the floor at her feet and leaned back against the bookcases.

"What are you doing?" she asked.

"I'm not leaving you."

"I'm going to be here all night."

"Then so am I."

She was silent a long time.

"This feels just like the night my parents died. The waiting. The sensation of time passing slowly, the hours stretching out as far as I can see. But at least I didn't cause this."

Nate frowned. "You didn't cause your parents' deaths either."

"That's not true. I killed my mother."

Frankie heard Nate's shocked breath and glanced at him. His big body was folded up on the floor, his capable hands resting on his knees. His face was filled with disbelief and sympathy.

She was so grateful for his presence because she wanted to talk. And for the first time in a decade, she let herself.

"When business at White Caps gradually decreased, my father took up refurbishing old sailboats. He'd always loved working with his hands. Alex used to help him. They did it in the barn out back. On the afternoon, my parents——" she couldn't say the word *died* so she kept going "——my father just finished one and had put it in the water to take it out for a test run. A storm blew up from the north. The bad weather came on fast and hard. It does that around here in the spring." She took a deep breath. "We found out later that the mast had snapped because it hadn't been reinforced properly. Evidently, he'd been struck on the head and swept into the lake."

Nate made a compassionate noise in the back of his throat.

"Did I tell you that I got into Middlebury on a swimming scholarship?" she said, afraid that if she stopped, she'd lose her courage. "I was a fantastic swimmer. All State. I could swim for miles and miles and Dad said that I took after him. That afternoon, I remember looking at the waves and thinking they were high, but not high enough to drown him. Not him. Not the man who could swim for fifty yards under water. I remember thinking that if the boat had gone over, he was swimming through those waves. To an island, to the shore. Towards home. Back to us."

She glanced out to the lake. "My mother and I waited for him to come back for at least an hour. There was more bad weather on the way so she called the sheriff's patrol, but they couldn't go after my Dad. They were busy rescuing a Boy Scout canoeing trip from the storm. So she headed for my father's fishing boat. It was just a tin can with an outboard motor on it. She told me to stay behind to watch Joy."

Frankie felt dizzy as she remembered the last time she'd seen her mother's face. Those lovely, kind eyes had been full of fear as she'd headed out into the lake, but she'd been bound and determined to get her husband.

"My mother couldn't swim. I knew she couldn't swim and I let her go out in a storm, in an unsafe little boat, with only a couple of flotation cushions. There was no life preserver. How much time would it have taken for me to run and get her a PFD from the house? We had them for the guests. God, I should have made her wait, I should have—" She could feel the hysteria rising in her chest.

"Frankie—"

She knew by the tone of his voice he was going to tell her it wasn't her fault and she cut him off. "Don't. Just don't. I grew up on this lake. I knew how it behaved. It was utterly irresponsible of me to let her go."

"But did it ever occur to you that you were not the parent?" Nate said gently. "That your mother was protecting her child by making you stay?"

Frankie closed her eyes. "All I know is that if I had gone, she'd be alive today. And Joy would have at least had a mother."

"You're putting a lot of responsibility on yourself."

"Who else can I put it on? When my mother took off, there was no one on that dock but me. Joy was in her room, scared to death. Alex wasn't home. I let my mother go." She shook her head. "I've replayed that moment when she went into that storm over and over again."

She dragged air into her lungs.

"I dream about that moment even now. Sometimes I'm the hero and I save them both. Sometimes she comes back with him. Most of the time, I'm just in the storm, waiting. Searching the rain." She looked down at him. "Kind of like right now."

Nate made a move to come forward, but she put her hands out. "If you hug me right now, I'm going to cry."

"So cry. I don't care." His arms were so good as they went around her. "Just don't ask me not to hold you."

An alarm was going off.

Frankie shifted uncomfortably. Her neck was stiff, her back was sore—

She flipped open her eyes.

She and Nate had slept on the floor of her office. And that wasn't an alarm, it was the phone.

She scrambled up to the desk and grabbed the receiver in the dark, thinking it must be two in the morning. "Hello?"

"Frances Moorehouse?"

Her throat tightened to the point of cutting off her air supply. She couldn't even respond.

"This is Commander Montgomery. Your brother's been found. He's injured and being treated at the local hospital for several broken bones. But he's alive and we're going to fly him home to you in forty-eight hours."

She clasped her hand over her mouth, tears starting to roll. Somehow, the commander ended the call and she replaced the receiver without dropping it. She launched herself into Nate's arms.

"He's alive. He's alive. He's alive…."

The following afternoon, Frankie finally got to talk with Alex. He was groggy from pain medication, but his hoarse voice was the sweetest thing she'd ever heard. Unfortunately, the Coast Guard was still looking for his partner, Reese Cutler. Alex was distraught about that, but he did seem to accept the fact that he had to come home to recuperate. As she hung up, she could just picture her brother trying to get out of a hospital bed so he could go and find his friend, even though he had casts on his leg and arm.

She got teary-eyed every time she thought of him and the near miss. Especially when she pictured Reese's wife still sitting by the phone.

As she and Alex had said goodbye, she'd told him that she'd get his old room ready for him. Just the thought of having him at White Caps for a little while was enough to put a smile on her face.

"So you've heard!"

Frankie looked up at the door. One of the guests was waving a newspaper and grinning.

"About what?" she asked.

"The review. In the *New York Times*." The man came forward and dropped the paper on her desk. The headline read, White Caps B & B: An Out of the Way Pleasure.

She laughed aloud. She'd never even known a critic, much less one working for the *Times*, had been through the dining room. "May I keep this?"

"Sure, as long as I'm guaranteed a table tonight."

She went into the kitchen to find Nate. He was making bread. "Did you see this?"

He looked up from the kneading. "Well, what do you know. Walter snuck in here."

"God, Nate. This could save us." She glanced away, reminding herself that they were not partners. "White Caps, I mean. Anyway, congratulations."

"Thanks. When are you going to pick up Alex at the airport?"

"Tomorrow afternoon."

"Want company?"

"I'll be fine. I'd like a little time alone with him, actually."

The truth was, though, she felt like pulling away from Nate. His support during those awful hours of waiting had been all that had gotten her through the night in one piece. She was grateful beyond measure, but she was so vulnerable to him now. He'd seen the very core of her.

And he was still leaving. In a month's time.

Needing some busy work to keep her mind off the future, she went to her office and re-ran her financial projections. If everything stayed the same, and with the *Times* article that was a pretty sure bet, they were going to make it, even with the accelerated deadline of August.

She refused to let herself think about the following summer. Maybe she'd be able to attract a better quality chef now that the restaurant had been written up. Maybe Nate would know someone who was of his caliber.

Yeah, like there were a whole bunch of French chefs who'd want to get pigeonholed in upstate New York.

It was a little before four when Nate's friend, Spike, called again. She left her desk to give them some privacy, and when she came back in from weeding the garden, they were still on the phone. A quick glance into the office showed Nate crouched over a legal pad, making notes and working her calculator.

The next day, Nate watched from the kitchen table as Frankie's Honda pulled up to the house and came to a gentle stop. She got out first but before she could make it around the car, the passenger side door opened wide. A pair of crutches emerged and then her brother carefully stood up.

Alex Moorehouse was a big man and built like an athlete, all wide shoulders and taut legs. His dark hair was short and streaked with blond, his skin was deeply tanned, and in the shorts and polo shirt he was wearing, he looked like an Abercrombie & Fitch model. His face, however, was all business, and as he shrugged off Frankie's attempt to help him, Nate could see that the two shared the same stubborn streak.

Nate got up and opened the door. As curious as he was about Frankie's brother, he was more interested in her. She seemed worried but pleased and he thought she was especially beautiful today, with her hair down and a light summer dress on.

When he looked back at her brother, Moorehouse's eyes had narrowed.

"This is our new chef, Nate. Nate, my brother Alex."

Moorehouse pegged the crutches into the ground and swiftly covered the distance to the door. Which meant he was either familiar with the damn things or just plain lithe.

Hell, it was probably both.

Nate offered his hand and Frankie's brother shook

it. Strong, firm grip. Nice enough nod. But the man's eyes were sending one very clear message: screw with my sister and I'll beat you to a pulp.

Nate could respect anyone who cared about Frankie, but he wasn't going to be pushed around, even if the poor guy had been through hell. So as soon as he had the chance, Nate made a point of putting his arm around Frankie. When she didn't pull away, he tucked her into his shoulder, gave her brother a long, level look and stood his ground.

Chapter Thirteen

Later that night, Frankie knew Alex had gotten bad news from the Coast Guard. The call came in just before seven, and when he limped out of her office, he went upstairs without stopping. He was never one to get emotional, certainly not in front of an audience, but his eyes had been bleak and unseeing as he'd passed by her. Reese Cutler was dead.

She let her brother go, even though she was sick with the thought of everything he insisted on dealing with alone.

As the dining room filled up, she took over hostess duties from Joy. It was hard to stay downstairs when all she wanted to do was try and talk with Alex, but Grand-Em was agitated by his return. It was as if his presence jangled her memory.

"Excuse me?"

Frankie snapped to attention at the sharp demand. "Sorry, er—"

Wow. The woman standing in front of her was a real beauty. Blond hair, haute couture pantsuit in white, blouse slit nearly to her belly button. She was city-slick, a real knockout, and she smelled good, too. Expensive and sexy.

"I'm here to see Nate." She shifted a briefcase to her other hand and checked a diamond watch.

"I'm sorry. He's busy." Really busy. Very, very busy.

"Tell him it's Mimi. And I want a table. Over there." She pointed to the windows that looked out over the lake. As luck would have it, there was a table for two open and no reason Ms. Fancy Pants couldn't have it.

Frankie picked up a menu and led *Mimi* across the room. The other diners snapped their necks to get a look at the blonde. It was like leading Vendala through a fraternity house.

After Mimi sat down, she picked up a fork and inspected the tines, as if looking for dirt. "Glass of Chardonnay. Not the house. I want something French. Is he making his escargot?"

"No."

"Then I want a salad." Mimi's eyes flashed. "He knows the way I like it."

Frankie's jaw tightened around her molars. The broad wasn't just talking about lettuce, she thought.

In a fierce mood, she stalked into the kitchen. Nate was flying over the stove, tossing spices and salt into four different sauté pans on the burners in front of him. Half-plated meals lined up behind him and more orders were getting put up by the waitresses.

"You've got a visitor," she said. "Right off Michael Kors's runway in New York. Mimi somebody."

Nate barely looked up. "Okay. Thanks."

"She wants a salad. Says you know how she likes it."

"Fine."

Frankie went over to where the wine was kept. She'd have felt so much better if he'd said something like, God, why's that horse-faced fashion victim darkening our door?

Of course, then he'd have to be referring to someone else entirely because there was nothing horse-faced about Mimi. And a man would have to be dead from the neck down not to want to have the blonde looking for him.

When Frankie went back out to the dining room, she was proud of herself. She'd only briefly considered slipping some rat poison into Mimi's French Chardonnay. And hadn't followed up on the impulse.

"Where is he?" the blonde demanded, as if she expected Nate to deliver the wine. "Did you tell him I'm waiting?"

"Yes."

Mimi smiled, although the joyless expression wasn't directed at Frankie. She was looking at the kitchen's doors. "Fine, but he better drop the defiant act when he starts next week."

"Starts what?"

Mimi's gaze shifted upwards, as if she was surprised to have to explain herself. "I'm the owner of Cosmos and he is my new Executive Chef."

Frankie narrowed her eyes. "Oh, really."

The woman looked around impatiently. "My salad? Where is it?"

"Coming right up." *Your Highness.*

Frankie marched into the kitchen.

Her first instinct was to jump in front of Nate and demand an explanation, but she held back. Hadn't she learned anything? The last couple of times she'd blown her lid off at him, she'd been in the wrong. She certainly owed him a chance to explain. Maybe there had been a misunderstanding. After all, he'd committed to stay until Labor Day so he had four weeks left.

She couldn't believe he'd break his promise and leave in seven days. That just wasn't like him.

Evidently, Mimi had perseverance as well as style and a lot of cash. The blonde waited all the way through until the end of the night. She wasn't gracious about the delay, but she didn't march into the kitchen and interrupt the flow of service, either.

Although maybe she was just determined to make Nate come to her.

Mimi also hated downtime, apparently. As soon as she'd polished off her salad, she got to work, spreading out papers and cracking open a laptop. When Frankie suggested she go to the library for some privacy, the woman missed the point and said she was fine with the noise. She didn't seem at all concerned that she was tying up a table, but Frankie wasn't about to cause a scene in front of her patrons by demanding Mimi go elsewhere.

At the end of the shift, Nate finally went out to talk with the woman. Frankie couldn't pretend to do any work while they were meeting so she cleaned her desk, filing loose inventory reports and accounting sheets, putting pens and pencils in the drawer, cleaning the phone. When there was nothing left to tidy, she picked up the *Times* review and sank back into her chair, reading it. She was cruising along, the words sinking in, when she frowned and had to backtrack.

* * *

Nathaniel Walker, black sheep of the wealthy and socially prominent Walker family, burst onto the culinary scene a decade ago. Following three years in Paris at Maxim's, the Walker heir returned to his family's seat in New York where he eventually landed at La Nuit....

The article went on, but she couldn't read anymore. The Walker heir.

Of course. Nate, short for Nathaniel.

Nathaniel Walker. The first man by that name had been a Revolutionary war hero and had signed the Declaration of Independence. Talk about American royalty. And wasn't a Walker now governor of Massachusetts? That was probably Nate's brother, who he'd said was into public service.

Hell, the Walkers were beyond rich. Made the Weatherbys look like candidates for a trailer park.

She threw the paper down. Boy, she knew how to pick them.

Good Lord, it was David all over again. Except this time, the man in question had lied about his family's wealth and influence, not been cowed by it.

Nate appeared in her doorway. "Hey, did you notice how busy we were tonight? Listen, about Mimi—"

"Yeah, let's talk about her. Thanks *so* much for giving me notice," Frankie snapped. What she was really angry about was the way he'd kept his family's identity from her, but Mimi sure as hell was a good target for the feelings of frustration and betrayal.

"Excuse me?"

"When we were you going to tell me you were leaving? The day before you took off?" Frankie planted her palms on the desk and shot up from her chair. "I can't believe you're pulling out in the middle of the season after you promised you'd stay until Labor Day!"

Nate put his hands on his hips and stared down at the floor like he was trying to control his temper.

"Look, Frankie—"

"God, I'm such a fool!" Her voice cracked. "I trusted you. I let you in. I'm so goddamned stupid."

"Frankie, I'm not going to the city next week. I'm staying here. You know what my plans are for the future. Hell, I want to include you in them. Come to New York with me."

"Yeah, and how's that going to work? Ms. Fancy Pants out there looked pretty damn handy with the back office stuff while she tied up one of my tables waiting for you."

"Mimi came up here to try and—"

"She'll make one hell of a partner, I'm sure—"

"Will you listen—"

"Although personally I think that blouse was a little low cut. Not for a stripper, of course—"

"Frankie—"

"Then again, she's more who I thought you'd go for—"

Nate pounded the desk with his fists, making paper clips bounce out of their holder. "Why the hell are you so concerned about who I'm going into business with! You're never going to leave this place. You'd rather hide behind your family than live your own life."

Frankie recoiled, but recovered quickly.

"Yeah, let's talk about family, why don't we?" She shoved the review at him. "Nathaniel Walker, heir to an American dynasty's fortune. When were you going to mention the fact that you've got more money than God? Or did you figure it'd be harder to get me into bed if I knew, considering I don't trust rich men—something which, incidentally, is proving to be a very accurate data screen for me."

Nate's face turned to stone, but his eyes blazed. "Did it ever occur to you that I didn't lie? Did you even for a *second* think—"

"So you're saying the *New York Times* fact-checker was taking a nap when this review went out?"

He leaned forward, over the desk. "Your lack of faith in me is astounding. But at least you're consistent."

With a bitter expletive, he turned around and headed for the door.

"Don't you dare put this on me!" She rushed across the room at him. "I asked you about your family. Twice. And this was after I'd made it clear what had happened with David. What the hell am I supposed to think when I find out the truth?"

Nate halted. His shoulders moved up and down while he breathed heavily.

"You just can't do it, can you," she muttered. "You just can't be honest."

Nate wheeled around so fast, she leaped back. His face was full of rage and pain.

"You want to know the *truth?*" He took angry steps towards her, forcing her to move backward. He looked as if he'd completely lost it. "I don't tell *anyone* about my family. And I'm not a Walker heir, I was disinherited by my father when I went to cooking school. My net worth is less than $100,000 and that's only because I've *busted my ass* and saved every dime I could."

She came up against the edge of the desk and gripped the wood.

Nate's voice wavered with emotion. "You want to know why I don't talk about them? Because I don't feel like a Walker. Because my parents rode me constantly for not being who they wanted me to be. But *mostly* it's because the last woman I told had an abortion when she found out I wasn't the rich man she thought I was."

Frankie felt the blood leave her face. "Oh, Nate—"

"My *child* was taken away from me. I was prepared to do the right thing when the woman told me she was pregnant, but then she got a look at the ring I could afford and split for some clinic." His body was shaking, his eyes too bright. "I hate my name. I hate where I come from. And to have you call me a liar because I didn't trot out my godforsaken lineage is a real frigging treat."

It all made such terrible sense. That night when they hadn't had a condom and he'd pulled away, shutting her out and looking haunted. The way he avoided children. His old car. His clothes. That he'd been hunting for months for a restaurant instead of just cutting a check for whatever caught his eye.

"I'm so sorry," she whispered.

Her voice seemed to reach him because he took a deep breath and collapsed into the chair in front of her desk.

"Ah, hell," he said, putting a hand up to his face.

"Nate, I had no idea."

He cursed, but at least he reached out for her hand. "Of course you didn't."

She stroked his shoulder. He was such a big man ordinarily, but he seemed to have shrunk into himself, his legs tucked under the chair, his arm wrapped around his stomach.

Anguish stretched his deep voice thin. "I keep thinking I'm going to get over it, you know? But every time I see some kid, I get hammered with what could have been. And, God, I blame myself."

"But you didn't make that choice. She did."

He talked over her. "I should have known. I should have fought, or something. I should have saved...I just didn't find out until it was too late."

"It wasn't your fault, Nate. It was a terrible tragedy and you lost something very, very real, but you are not responsible."

He looked up from between his fingers. His eyes were shiny.

"You are not responsible," she repeated.

"And this is coming from you?" he countered gently.

Frankie thought of her mother disappearing into the storm. "That was different."

"How?"

"I don't know."

"Because it happened to you?"

"Maybe."

He tugged her down so she was sitting in his lap. "It's so much easier to forgive other people, isn't it. It's harder when it comes to ourselves."

She nodded slowly.

They stayed that way for a long time.

"I'm not going to work for Mimi," he said abruptly. "I'd already told her no in the spring. When she saw the piece in the *Times,* she figured she'd try and persuade me again. I was direct with her. There's no way I'm going to be sidetracked, even by the likes of Cosmos."

Frankie cleared her throat. "What if you don't find something to buy? What will you do?" The real thing she wanted to know was whether there was any chance he'd consider staying.

"I'm just going to keep looking. I don't care if it takes a decade," he said forcefully. "I've had to fight for what I wanted all my life. My parents never respected me because I was supposed to be a lawyer or a finance guy like my brother. I was supposed to marry a debutante and have two towheaded children and live in Wellesley and belong to the club and play racquetball. But I was always different. My friends were metalheads who had tattoos. I didn't go out for crew, I played hockey and got my nose broken and my front tooth knocked out. I barely made it through Harvard, not because I couldn't do the work, but because I didn't care."

She smoothed his hair back, drinking in what he was saying. The answers to her questions were tumbling out of him, filling in the blanks.

"I can't give up. I won't give up. Because if I have my own place, I succeed or fail on my own. No one tells me what to do unless I ask for their advice. And no one can take it away from me."

"You're going to get what you want," she said, aware that her heart was breaking. For him. For them. Their split was inevitable and it was coming so fast. Four weeks.

Make them count, she thought.

His eyes flashed up to hers. He had such beautiful eyes. Green and gold.

"I meant what I said, Frankie. I want you to come with me. You'd be fantastic and I know we can work together."

She kissed him on the forehead. "Shh."

He captured her hands. "I phrased it badly before, but you really can't live your life for your family. Staying here and working yourself to the bone isn't going to bring your parents back."

She stood up and he let her go. "I know that."

"Do you?" he prompted quietly.

Going over to a window, she looked out at the lake. She couldn't expect him to understand. He'd turned his back on his family because they couldn't accept who he was. Worse, he'd been burned tragically by his association with the Walker name. So there was little possibility he could appreciate how much her sister and Grand-Em and White Caps meant to her.

But then his words came back to her. If she lived her life only for her family, what did she really have that was her own?

Hell, maybe she was the one with the problem. Maybe she was totally blinded by the past. Incapable of seeing her future.

"Frankie, I'm not sure you get it."

"Maybe you're right."

And for the first time, she tried to peel away from her vow to her sister and her responsibility for Grand-Em and the weight of keeping White Caps going. She just breathed in and out while staring at the water, trying to let go of her regrets.

Knowledge came slowly, but it was the deep kind, the in-your-soul kind. White Caps wasn't just home, a relic to her family. It was also where she herself belonged.

She turned around. "The thing is, I love it here. I truly do. I might have some fantasy about what life in the big city would be like, but the thrill of that would pass. When I was younger, when I was with David, it was different. *I* was different. But I've found my rhythm, I really have. And it's in the seasons of this place."

How funny that she was just figuring that out now. Tonight.

"I don't want to stop seeing you," he said, staring at her hard.

She closed her eyes. So it wasn't just business for him, not just casual sex. She felt the bones in her body loosen and realized she'd been carrying around so much tension. There had been so many words unspoken, feelings unrevealed. Until now.

"Oh, Nate. I don't want things to end, either."

She heard him rise from the chair, the wood creaking as his weight was lifted.

"I didn't expect to get emotionally attached to you," he said in his deep voice. God, she loved that rumbling sound.

She looked up at him. "Neither did I."

He smiled and bent down, his lips brushing hers. "You know, there's an express train that runs from Albany to New York."

"And planes fly back and forth all the time," she murmured.

He kissed her and she eased against his body. He was so solid, so warm, his arms tightening around her, holding her close.

But even as she said the words, she knew she didn't believe in their future. Long distance was hard, especially when one person was starting a whole new business. And the other was trying to keep an old one afloat. Distance meant stilted phone calls and missed connections and messages left on machines. It meant exhausted conversations at the end of hard nights. And gradual loss.

She'd been through it before. And though Nate was nothing like David, the toll would be taken. In the real world, daily life was inexorable, capable of wearing away the best of intentions, the most ardent of hearts, like water over stone.

He pulled back. "You look grim."

She smoothed his cheek with her palm. "Let's not talk about the future. Take me upstairs to my bed and make love to me."

Nate stared up at the ceiling as Frankie slept.

He had told no one about Celia. Even Spike didn't have the full story.

He'd kept what had happened to himself because it hurt to put words to the events. And because he so regretted not having read the situation better. He should have known by the disgusted look on Celia's face when he'd told her he wasn't a wealthy guy that she was capable of doing something awful. He'd just assumed that because she wasn't a rich man's daughter that she wouldn't care about money.

A fatal miscalculation.

Absently, he stroked Frankie's arm. She'd been so damn supportive. But she was like that. Loyal. Fiercely protective of those she cared about.

She reminded him of Spike.

He thought about his friend and their plans. While Frankie had been out in the garden weeding this afternoon, Spike had called with bad news. The place they'd been talking about hadn't panned out because they just couldn't make the money work. It would be a terrible mistake to try and get a new joint off the ground while being too strapped with debt.

Nate knew what they were up against. Ninety percent of new restaurants closed their doors within a year. But if his first attempt didn't work, he was prepared to whore himself out to a celebrity joint for the next five years, amass another nest egg and try again. Spike was likewise too pigheaded to take failure seriously.

God, they'd waited so long to make their mark. They'd sweated over blistering hot stoves and flaming grills, had worked double and triple shifts through burned hands and backs that ached. They'd honed their craft and paid their dues.

Their shot was going to come. It just had to.

Frankie stirred in her sleep, letting out a soft sigh of contentment as she snuggled in close.

Nate closed his eyes. When she'd told him she didn't want to talk about the future, he'd known exactly what the bleak expression on her face had meant. She was a realist, not a romantic. And she knew what it took to be in business for yourself. You didn't have a lot of discretionary time for outside relationships. Especially long distance ones.

As he thought about the future, Labor Day loomed on the horizon like a thief. Leaving Frankie was going to be hard.

Nate turned his head and breathed in the scent of her shampoo and her skin.

Leaving Frankie was going to kill him.

Chapter Fourteen

The next morning, Frankie knocked softly on her brother's door. "Alex?"

The response was slow in coming, delivered in a low tone. "Yeah."

She shifted the tray in her hand. "I brought you a little breakfast."

There was a grunt and a shuffling sound. The door opened.

His beard had grown in overnight, darkening his jaw and cheeks, and his hair was roughed up. He had on a pair of shorts that hung off his hips and there were bruises on his chest, black and blue ones dark enough to show through his tan.

"Thanks." He took the tray, but didn't invite her in.

She watched with a hollow pit in her stomach as he put the food down on the bureau and limped back to bed. He was too big for the twin mattress, his feet hanging off the end, and he seemed equally out of place in the room. The America's Cup posters of his teenage years had faded, the model ships he'd built with their father had sagging sails now. He was a man in a boy's space and it struck her as odd that she'd never thought of redecorating his room. Although it wasn't as if she'd had the money.

And she supposed a part of her had wanted to keep it as it was. The remains of a brother she never really expected to come back home.

"Do you need anything?" She stepped inside and that was when she saw a bottle of scotch on the floor, within easy reach of his hand. It was half empty.

He eyed her darkly as if he didn't want her to come any closer. "Nope."

The answer wasn't a surprise, and since bringing him something to eat hadn't been the only reason she'd come, she wasn't going to pussyfoot around. He appeared on the verge of ordering her out the door. "Do you need help getting to the funeral?"

He looked away, to one of the windows. "No."

"When is it?"

"I don't know."

"Have you talked to Reese's wife?"

"Widow. Cassandra's a widow now."

Frankie closed her eyes. Reese Cutler had been Alex's partner for years and she'd met the man once or twice. He was—*had been*—an industrial engineer who'd made millions and millions building manufacturing plants for the likes of Ford and GM. His widow, Cassandra, had been his second wife and nearly half his age, if Frankie remembered correctly.

"I'm sure she'd appreciate hearing from you."

Alex's voice was bitter. "Yeah, if I were her, I'd be in a big hurry to talk to me."

"Weren't you friends?"

"Frankie, don't take this the wrong way, but back off, okay?" His face contorted as he moved the leg with the cast to another position.

She cleared her throat. "I'm sorry that it took…what happened to get you home. But I'm so glad you're here and I hope you'll stay for a while. I've missed you. Joy has, too. You were always her hero."

"She needs to pick a new one."

"Alex, we love you. Please remember that."

Not expecting a response, she headed for the door.

"Frankie?"

She glanced over her shoulder. His head was still turned to the wall.

"I have to go to the orthopedic surgeon. They want me eval'ed for surgery on my leg. The bone might have to be replaced by a metal rod."

She winced and wondered what that would do to his sailing career. "When?"

"Tomorrow afternoon in Albany. Can you take me?"

"Of course."

"Thanks."

She closed the door.

"How's he doing?" Nate asked from the head of the stairs.

"Not well, but I don't know how badly. He's not a big talker."

They went down to the kitchen.

"Would you mind coming with us to Albany tomorrow?" she asked. "He has to get his leg looked at. To be honest, I'm a fainter when it comes to mixing family with physicians. When Joy had her wisdom teeth out in the hospital, I hit the floor twice."

Nate kissed her. "No problem. I'm glad you asked."

Alex opened his eyes the moment the door closed. Frankie's concern was well-intended, but it rubbed him raw.

There was no way in hell he was going to the funeral. He wanted to pay his respects, but he just couldn't look Cassandra in the face. Then again, he never really had been able to do that.

Which was what happened when you fell in love with your best friend's wife.

God, Cassandra. He could remember so clearly the first moment he saw her. He and Reese had been coming in from a race down to Bermuda and back. As they'd pulled into the Narragansett Bay Yacht Club's dock, Reese had waved at a woman who was jogging lithely toward them.

"That's my wife," he'd said with pride.

"When did you get married again?" Alex had asked.

"Haven't done the ceremony yet, but she's my wife all right. And I'm going to make this one stick."

Alex had had an impression of long red hair and a perfectly proportioned female body, but that was as far as he got. As she'd leaped up into Reese's arms, he'd looked away as a shock of pure lust and heat shot through him.

That day, that moment of seeing her in the setting sun, her hair flashing copper in the fading light, had marked him. He'd never understood how it was possible to be obsessed with someone you didn't know, but then it had happened to him.

Over the years, he'd learned more about Cassandra, though he'd never prompted his friend to talk. Reese had spoken easily enough and on his own about his wife. There had been plenty of stories about her accomplishments as an architect, the parties she threw, the small, intimate things she did. And Alex had only wanted more of the peeks into her world, even though he'd felt like hell obsessing about her. It had been so hard to be reduced to a voyeur, a greedy, sneaky bastard who was a parasite on someone else's marriage. The guilt had been tremendous.

And then it had all gotten worse.

He'd thought he was alone on the boat. He'd honestly believed Reese and Cassandra had left. Which was the only reason he'd stepped out into the cabin, naked and drying his hair with a towel after a shower.

When a shocked gasp behind him cut through his solitude, he'd looked over his shoulder. Cassandra was in the galley kitchen, in the midst of filling up a glass with lemonade. As her eyes had traveled down his body, she'd spilled the stuff all over the counter.

God, even now the memory of her stare was enough to stir him.

As he'd cursed and covered his ass with the towel, she'd stammered an apology, but he hadn't heard much of it. All he'd been thinking of was, thank God he hadn't turned around. Because then she would have seen the monstrous erection that had popped up the instant she'd looked at him.

He'd gone back into the head, braced his arms on the tiny sink and tried to remember how to breathe. When he'd come back out ten minutes later, she was gone. And after that, he'd quickly changed the subject whenever

Reese had talked about her. At one point, a couple months later, his friend had asked him whether or not he had a problem with Cassandra. Alex had prevaricated and Reese had never brought her up again.

In the information vacuum, Alex had hoped to lose interest, but his fixation hadn't needed fresh news or sightings to thrive. He'd continued to think of her, particularly at sunset when he was out on the ocean and the tips of the waves were tinted the color of copper.

And his guilt, like his obsession, had continued to burn.

He knew she was a fantasy. She had to be. No one was as perfect as the image he'd constructed in his mind.

But he wasn't ever going to find out the truth of who she was. How she kissed. How she made love. As far as he was concerned, Reese's widow was as untouchable as Reese's wife had been.

Especially considering what had happened out in that storm.

Alex squeezed his eyes shut again. Grief radiated out of his chest, running through his veins like vinegar, drowning out the aches in his body. He gritted his teeth so he didn't cry out like a sissy, but tears escaped, rolling down his cheeks like the salty spray of the sea.

Nate was hotter than hell in the kitchen. He'd finished with his daily prep, the bread was made, and he had an hour before he had to get dinner service rolling. He took the back stairs two at a time, changed into his bathing suit, and went to look for Frankie. He found her in the garden, bent over, staking up the tomato plants. He took a moment to admire her long legs.

"You want to go for a swim?" he asked.

She glanced at him from under her arm and smiled. Tendrils of hair were curling around the nape of her neck from the heat and her sweat. "Great idea. I've got three more to go. I'll meet you down at the lake."

As he looked into the flashing blue of her eyes, a shaft of yearning pierced his heart.

"Go on, now. Shoo," she said laughingly. "You're distracting me."

"If you need any help getting into your bathing suit, let me know."

"Maybe you can get me out of it after we're done swimming."

"Lady, it would be my pleasure."

He ambled down the lawn. When he got to the end of the dock, he jumped into the water, feeling the cooling rush over his skin. He floated on his back, sculling with his hands, staring up at the blue sky and the white clouds and the blinding yellow sunlight.

"Hey, mister?"

Nate looked over to the right. There was a seven-year-old boy standing at the shore, a brilliant orange life jacket hanging cockeyed from his little body.

"Mister, can you help me? I'm not allowed to go on the dock without this thing, but I can't get the things right and if I don't get them right my brother's going to tell on me because I put toothpaste in his shoe last night, and I want to see the fish because they were there yesterday and I need to know if they are still there and I can't see them from the shore—"

Nate blinked and treaded water as the sentence went on and on.

It ended with, "So will you, huh? Please?"

Nate looked around. There were no other grown-ups in sight so he swam over to the dock's ladder, climbed out of the water, and dried off his face and hands. He approached cautiously, like the kid was of a different species entirely and maybe of the stinging variety. He fiddled with the straps and snap hooks, got everything where it should be, and rose to his feet. It was like passing a test, he thought.

"Thanks, mister. My name is Henry. I come from New York City. I'm six and a half. My brother's nine and he's a pain, but I kind of like him sometimes except when he's mean, which is not really all that often. My mother says she's happy that she had two boys but that she doesn't want any more kids, which is too bad because I want a sister…"

Henry followed Nate back out to the end of the dock, chattering all the way. When they got to the end, Nate sat down and the boy plopped right next to him. Which was not exactly what Nate had had in mind.

"Although, I don't know, maybe she wouldn't like SpongeBob SquarePants and then I don't know if I would like her and I wonder whether there would be fewer presents…"

Nate couldn't help but stare at the kid. He had rosy cheeks and bright green eyes and his hands flew around as he talked like a sparrow's wings.

"Do you?" Henry demanded.

Nate shook himself. "I'm sorry, what?"

"Know anything about fish?"

"Ah, yeah."

There was a pause and Nate had to wonder if Henry was finally oxygenating his blood. The kid hadn't taken more than two breaths since he'd stepped off the grass.

"So?" Came the sturdy prompt. "Whadayaknow about them?"

Nate cleared his throat. And then something odd happened. He started telling Henry about the different ways a chef could cook fish and before he knew it they were in a conversation.

Henry was a sponge, all rapt eyes and smart questions. The kid was going to grow up to be an intellectual and that maybe explained why his head seemed so large on his thin shoulders. He probably needed extra room for that brain of his.

When footsteps approached, Nate looked over his shoulder.

Thank God, replacement troops.

"Hi," Frankie said gently. Her voice was even, but her eyes were concerned, as if she feared he'd been trapped by the boy. "What's going on?"

Henry looked up. "Hi. I'm Henry, I met you yesterday, remember? I'm learning about fish. Did you know that he's a chef?"

Frankie smiled. "Yes, I did."

"He knows everything about fish."

"Does he?"

Henry nodded gravely, as if he were a medical resident who'd had the chance to spend time with Jonas Salk.

Frankie looked back at Nate and he gave her a small smile. He couldn't say that being with Henry was easy. But it wasn't painful, either, probably because he was so distracted by all the talk. And the weird thing was, he kind of liked passing what he knew along to such a captivated audience.

Frankie sat down on the other side of Henry, dangling her bare feet in the water. Nate stared across the boy's dark head at her. She had a grin on her face while she listened to Henry regurgitate what he'd learned, like a little tape recorder.

Unexpectedly, Nate felt the urge to laugh as his own words drifted out into the summer air, spoken in a much higher octave and with a slight lisp.

At the end of the night, Frankie turned off her desk lamp. Nate had gone upstairs already and she could hear him moving around above her. She sat in the dark for a few minutes, just listening to him.

Sitting on that dock with Henry between them had been a joy and a torment. She could tell Nate had felt awkward because his voice had been strained and his back stiff. But by the time the boy's mother had called him inside to change for dinner, Frankie could have sworn Nate was almost enjoying himself. That was the good part.

The more awkward thing was that the scene made her think of having a child with him. She just couldn't help testing the fantasy and seeing if it fit. And boy, did it ever.

Well, at least in her mind it did.

Except he'd already told her he didn't want marriage or a family and one conversation with a seven-year-old about ichthyology wasn't going to change all that.

And hell, even if he did want to get down on one knee, and he'd given her no reason to expect that he ever would for anybody, there was still the little inconvenience of them being separated by *hundreds* of miles.

Frankie went upstairs and got into the shower, thinking she needed to get away from her morose thoughts. The water pressure was pathetic, barely enough to get the suds out of her hair, and she wondered whether Alex was out of bed. Maybe now that the house was quiet, he'd ventured from his room and was washing his hair in the sink or taking a sponge bath.

When she got to her room, Nate was in bed. His book was open on his lap, but his head was back against the pillows and his eyes were closed. With his cheekbones even more prominent than usual, he looked exhausted and as if he'd lost some weight. He'd been working so hard in that hot kitchen and they'd been... busy during the nights. Although she was also tired, from Alex's disappearance and worrying about the business, at least she hadn't had to cook a hundred meals every night on top of it all.

She tiptoed over to him, slid the book from his hands and turned off the lamp. As she got in next to him, he let out an unintelligible sentence, dragged her body as close to his as he could get it, and started to snore softly. She'd gotten used to the sounds he made. To the way his body weighted down the mattress so she always ended up in a hole next him. To his warmth and his smell.

With cold dread, she imagined herself having to adjust to sleeping without him.

Hours later, she must have had some kind of nightmare. She woke up in the early morning, damp with sweat, tears on her face. Nate was stroking her hair, looking worried. When she reached for him, they made love—the sweet, slow gentle kind.

They were laying together, with her body draped boneless and utterly satisfied over his, when he asked her what her dream had been about.

"I don't know." She stroked his chest. "I think I was in an old house. Going from room to room. There was someone I was supposed to find, but I just couldn't get to them."

"I've had dreams like that. The searching variety. I had a lot of them after…" He hesitated. "After Celia left."

Celia. Her name had been Celia.

Frankie was tempted to ask all sorts of questions, but what was the point? The events had marked him and doing a postmortem on what had caused the scars wasn't going to change anything.

Instead, she found herself wanting to tell him that she loved him.

The realization that she had fallen for him didn't really seem sudden or out of the blue. It had been emerging for a time, slowly inching free of her unconsciousness, coming to the forefront of her mind.

She loved him.

The words were so close to breaching her lips, carried up out of her heart on a complicated wave of awe and bittersweet sorrow. So her mouth would stay closed, she kissed him, and lingered, keeping their lips together.

Chapter Fifteen

Nate had just gone down to start breakfast when Frankie thought she heard him cursing. She froze, her pants halfway up her legs. Yup, that low rumble was him letting loose a few good ones. Yanking a shirt on over her head and throwing on some shoes, she quickly descended the stairs and nearly tripped on her own feet when she walked into the kitchen.

At first, she couldn't even comprehend what she was looking at.

There were two inches of water across the floor and more was coming in from a huge hole in the ceiling. Sheetrock covered the stove and the counters.

"Oh, my God," she breathed in horror.

Nate climb up onto a countertop and peered into the rafters. "A pipe must have burst hours ago and the damn thing has to be hooked into the supply line. You need time and a constant supply of water to make this kind of mess."

Of course. Her shower last night. No pressure.

"You better check the walk-in," Nate said. "If the compressor got wet, it's probably shorted out."

She crossed the room, splashing as she went, the water soaking into her sneakers. Sure enough, the compressor wasn't working and there was a faint burning smell in the air.

This cannot be happening, she thought. It just couldn't be real. Any minute now the alarm clock was going to go off and they'd have a chuckle about her vivid imagination.

Any minute.

A sloshing noise cut through her stupid optimism.

George looked worried as he came into the room. "I turned the sink off last night. Really, I did. At least I think I did."

Hearing his voice helped her flip into crisis mode. She went to her office and called the plumber and the electrician. When she came back to the kitchen, Nate had gotten out mops and buckets, but was shaking his head.

"We need a water pump. Is there a U-Rent-It place around here?"

She got lost for a moment looking into the rafters. Water was relentlessly snaking into her house. How much was this going to cost to repair? Thousands. Tens of thousands. Her stomach rolled. She had a home owner's insurance policy, but old, rotting plumbing fell into the act of God category.

Actually, those rotting pipes were more like Lucifer's territory.

"Frankie?"

"Ah, there's one in the next town over. The plumber said he'd be here in fifteen minutes. If you can watch him, I'll go and get the equipment."

Nate nodded. "This doesn't smell like sewage, but the crud in that ceiling is nasty. I'm going to have to disinfect everything before we can serve food out of here. You should assume we're closed down at least until tomorrow afternoon. Probably longer."

She thought of all the income they were going to lose. The guests were going to be due a refund for some of their payments. White Caps was a bed and *breakfast* after all. And they'd been making money hand over fist in the dining room, but that was going to stop, effective immediately.

As Frankie stared at the dirty puddle she was standing in, she realized it was all over. There was no way to meet the mortgage payments now. White Caps was lost.

She must have moaned or something because suddenly Nate was pulling her into his shoulder. As all of the fight left her, the only thing keeping her standing was his strong arm around her waist.

Joy waved as the Honda drove off. It had taken a half hour to convince Frankie that she could leave with Alex and Nate to go see the orthopedic surgeon and everything would still be under control. Because truly, there was nothing to be done. The plumber had shut off the water supply at the source and determined that the whole pipe system in the back end of the house needed to be replaced. The only good news was that he'd been able to jerry-rig a way for the bathrooms in the front to get water so the guests were taken care of.

Reservations for the dining room had been cancelled

indefinitely. Between replacing the walk-in compressor, installing the new plumbing and putting up fresh Sheetrock, they'd be lucky to reopen the kitchen in a week. But at least Frankie was handling the whole thing really well. She was utterly calm, even when the plumber had told her his part of the job would be upwards of $15,000. Assuming everything went smoothly.

Joy headed back inside. The guests were eating lunch in town, George had gone upstairs for a nap, and Grand-Em was in her room, rereading the dance cards from her 1939 debut at the Plaza in New York. For Joy, having a few moments to herself was an incredible luxury and she decided to take a swim.

After changing into her bikini, she went down to the dock and was about to dive in when she heard her name being called.

That voice. *His* voice.

She turned around and squinted into the sun, thinking she had to be hallucinating.

But good Lord, was that Gray Bennett? Walking down the lawn to her?

Joy lunged for her towel and wrapped it around herself. Being practically naked in front of him was not going to improve her verbal skills.

Which had pretty much drained out of the soles of her feet and into the cribbing anyway.

God, he was too beautiful to look at. Dressed in tennis whites and with his dark hair all shiny in the sunlight, he looked powerful and sexy. With his sunglasses hiding his eyes, he seemed calm and in control, but she was curious to find as he got closer that his harsh, hawklike face was somewhat tense.

"Where is everyone?" he asked as he hit the dock.

She opened her mouth and words came out in a ramble. "We had a little plumbing problem in the kitchen so the guests are out to lunch and Frankie took my brother to Albany."

"Alex is in town?"

"He was in an accident."

Gray frowned and took off the glasses. His blue eyes glowed with intelligence. "I'm sorry to hear that. Is he all right?"

"We hope he will be. What are you doing here?" She winced. Way to be welcoming. Maybe she should kick him in the shins while she was at it. "What I mean is—"

He smiled. "My father's birthday is in the middle of September and we're going to have the party up here this year. I was wondering if White Caps catered."

They never had before, but she couldn't imagine Frankie would turn down business, especially now. "Why don't I have my sister give you a call?"

"Sounds good." He put his sunglasses back on and his head tilted down a little. As crazy as it was, she had the feeling he was staring at her. And that he'd covered his eyes because he didn't want her to know it.

"Mind if I ask you something?" he said.

Her breath caught. "Sure."

And let's hope it's out to dinner, she thought.

"How old are you?"

"Twenty-seven."

"I remember being twenty-seven. It's a great age."

As if he had decades on her.

Joy scowled. "Yeah, well, I feel like I'm forty."

Because being in the full-time, eldercare business would do that to a person.

"Well, you don't look it," he said dryly. "Not even close. You could barely pass for your own age."

The idea he thought she was overly young rankled and she looked away from his too handsome face. Unfortunately, her eyes latched on to his legs. His thighs were striated with muscle and so were his calves. Fine dark hair marked his tanned skin.

With the force of a sucker punch, she was hit by a wild, illicit fantasy of what one of those thighs would feel like parting her knees and then brushing up against her core as he kissed her deep and hard. Her body roared to life, blood pumping, lungs getting tight.

And had someone poured warm honey all over her skin?

"It was nice seeing you again, Joy." Gray's voice was professional-sounding, as if he were dismissing her.

"Can I ask you a question?" she blurted.

His eyebrows arched over the top of the sunglasses. "Fair's fair."

"Why do you want to know how old I am?"

He didn't miss a beat. "Actually, I was curious about Frankie. She's handling this place really well, but I figure she's only what, three years older than you?"

The fact that he'd only wanted to know about her sister put the kibosh on her inner harlot. Quick as a cold shower, she was back to normal. "Yes. Yes, she is."

"I look forward to her call. And I'm sure your kitchen will be back up and running in no time. Your plumber's working damn hard."

Joy frowned. The plumber had already left.

"Although by the sound of it, he's also a demolition expert." Gray waved and turned away.

She watched him saunter down the dock. He moved smoothly and powerfully. She wanted to call him back. To ask him to swim with her or just to stay and talk about anything. Her sister. His father's party. The weather.

And then, as if he'd heard her wish, he stopped just as he reached the grass. "Your brother," he said over his shoulder.

"What about him?" She tugged up the edge of her towel.

There was a pause and then he seemed to shake himself to attention. "The accident. Was it on Reese Cutler's sailboat?"

"Yes, it was. Did you know Alex's partner?"

"His wife, Cassandra, actually. Is Reese okay?"

"I'm so sorry," she said gently. "He was killed."

Gray swore under his breath. "That's awful. I'm sure Alex is devastated."

"He is."

"If there's anything I can do, let me know."

"We will."

He nodded his goodbye and strode up the lawn. His concern for her brother touched her heart, draining away some of the frustration. And as if panning for gold, she replayed their conversation, something she always did whenever they said even two words to each other. Something struck her. If he'd cared about how old Frankie was, why hadn't he just come out and asked *her* age?

And what was that thing about the plumber?

Joy hurried up to the house, and as she got closer, she heard a loud thumping sound. Coming from upstairs. Confused, she followed the sounds to the Lincoln Bedroom.

And jerked to a halt in the doorway.

George was driving a sledgehammer into the wall while Grand-Em stood next to him with great satisfaction.

"What are you doing!" Joy hollered.

Gray Bennett slid into his BMW and gripped the steering wheel hard enough to turn his knuckles white.

He felt like a lecher. Ogling some woman—some *girl* like that.

Damn it, even though she'd said she felt like she was forty, Joy Moorehouse looked like she was barely out of high school. All lovely skin and luscious strawberry blond hair and flashing eyes—that special, rare innocence drifting off of her like sweet perfume.

She made him feel ancient.

And hot as hell.

He groaned, shifting in the leather seat. What the hell was he doing, fantasizing about Joy Moorehouse? He'd known her forever. Good God, he could remember her in pigtails as she'd danced across the grass of the town square during some parade or other. And he'd always thought she was lovely, sure, but this summer, something had changed. He'd first noticed the difference when he'd seen her sitting in a car downtown in early July. He'd been struck by her smile as she'd spoken to her grandmother. It was so honest. Direct. Uncomplicated.

And just now while he'd looked into those wide, beautiful eyes of hers, he'd somehow been reminded of every dirty deed he'd ever done in his life. All the way back to when he'd stolen a BB gun from the Saranac Lake hardware store when he was eleven.

God, the list of bad things he'd done was a long one. Which was what you'd expect from a political operative who'd floated around the Washington cesspool for a decade and a half.

Dens of iniquity just did not spawn men of honor, he thought. And the righteous never survived in them.

Politics was all about playing hardball and he had one hell of a vicious arm, as well as a fantastic accuracy rate. Which was why he was paid so damn well and feared by public servants all the way up the food chain into the Oval Office itself. He'd made a fortune, to add to the one he'd inherited, and for a long time, he'd been downright impressed with himself.

Lately, though, he'd begun to feel that he'd lost his way. Lost himself. And seeing Joy brought those dislocations into close, painful focus. He'd wanted to reach out and touch a little of her purity, as if that would cleanse him.

He gritted his teeth and thought there was going to be absolutely no touching.

Sweet, innocent girls were not safe with the likes of him. He'd broken enough hearts to know that his attractions were intense and short-lived. He moved on as soon as he got what he wanted, and though he didn't like his behavior, he hadn't been able to break the pattern and he wasn't into lying. No woman had captured his attention for long, and when they asked him how he felt, he was honest.

Which had led him to being slapped once or twice.

He closed his eyes. And saw Joy standing on the dock before she'd become aware of his presence, that bikini of hers giving nearly everything away.

Gray cursed and started the car. All he needed was to be caught sitting in her driveway staring into space with a hard-on. Yeah, that would be just terrific.

As he headed out onto Route 22, he told himself that as soon as he and his father headed back to Washington, everything would return to normal. He'd forget all about those wide, lovely eyes of hers. Within days of being in D.C., he wouldn't think of her at all.

Frankie let Nate drive home from Albany because she was exhausted and distracted. As they got on the Northway, she glanced over her shoulder once again.

Alex was out cold in the back of the car. After all the tests the doctors had put him through, he looked like he'd been to hell and back, his skin sallow under his tan, his eyes sunken. His whole body had been shaky as he'd gotten out of the hospital's wheelchair and maneuvered himself into the back seat at the end of the ordeal. The orthopedic surgeon had decided to operate on his leg and ankle next week and his recovery was going to be a long and very expensive one.

Thank God he'd been smart enough to get himself health-care coverage a few years ago.

Frankie reached out to stroke his arm, but held back, not wanting to wake him. Although it had been hard to see him suffer through all those tests, what pained her more than anything else was how unclear his future was. It was hard to tell whether or not his career as a professional sailor was over. She thought he suspected it was, however, and that the loss must be staggering.

"Is he asleep?" Nate asked.

She nodded and settled back into her seat.

"Listen," Nate continued, "I've been thinking about the kitchen situation."

So had she. The disaster had been in the back of her mind all afternoon. As had its implications.

"I'm selling," she said softly.

His head jacked around. "What?"

"You heard me."

"Why?"

"Why the hell do you think? I'm out of money," she snapped. With a ragged breath, she put a hand to her forehead and leaned against the window. "I'm sorry."

Nate's palm, warm and sure, covered her knee. "We can make it. I'll get us back up and rolling as soon as I can."

She squeezed her eyes shut. "Don't say we. Please just...don't."

His touch evaporated.

"I want to help you," he said with an edge.

"I know you do." *But you're leaving in three weeks.* "Except it really is over. I called Mike Roy before we left and told him to get in touch with the Englishman."

"Ah, hell, Frankie." Nate's voice was rough.

"It's my only option. Even if I could afford to replace the plumbing, there are a hundred other things in that house that are on the verge of exploding. White Caps needs someone who can make a serious capital investment. We're talking hundreds of thousands of dollars. And besides, even if I could squeak by on the mortgage this year, I've got a huge tax bill to face in the spring. This season's business was...extraordinary, thanks to you. But next year? We're not going to be able to sustain the momentum. I need to face reality."

And it was breaking her heart.

Her conversation with Mike had been short, but grueling. And in spite of the fact that he hadn't been totally up front with her about Karl Graves, she knew he felt awful.

"There has to be a way," Nate said.

"There isn't. And I have to accept that so please don't…don't try and give me hope."

Nate's jaw tightened as he fell silent.

When they finally pulled into White Caps' driveway, dusk was draining the light from the sky and the house glowed. Nate killed the engine, but Frankie made no move to get out of the car. She just stared at her home.

Images flooded her mind, wrenching her back to the past. She saw her family together on the side lawn at Alex's thirteenth birthday party. And her father sticking his head out an upstairs window while launching a balsa wood glider into the air. She remembered snowmen being rolled in the winter, and fireflies getting caught in the summer, and the brilliant leaves falling in the autumn.

At least she could take the memories with her, though they would be less vivid somehow.

She looked at her brother in the back seat. Alex's long arms and legs were stretched out, the casts very white against his tanned skin. A pillow was crammed against one door, his head bent at an angle.

"I just don't know how to tell them," she whispered before reaching out and gently touching her brother's forearm. "Lexi? Lexi, we're home."

His lids lifted and those brilliant blue eyes were horribly dull. As he struggled to sit up, he refused the hand she offered.

"Frankie!" Joy burst out of the house. "Frankie! You're not going to believe this! Guess what!"

The roof caved in, Frankie thought numbly. No, wait, the roof let go *and* the front staircase collapsed.

She got out of the car, not paying too much attention to Joy. She was more concerned with getting Alex to his feet without having him fall over. And naturally, he was busy pushing her away.

"Frankie!" Joy thrust something in her face. "Look at this!"

She forced her tired eyes to focus.

On a diamond ring the size of a walnut.

"Nice piece of bling," Alex muttered as he arranged himself on his crutches and started slowly for the house.

"What the hell is that?" Frankie demanded.

"Grand-Em and George found it. In the wall. Arthur Garrison really did give it to her and she really did hide it from her father so he couldn't make her accept the proposal."

"My…God." Frankie took the piece. It was heavy and sparkled like a rainbow.

"We can pay for the plumbing with it!" Joy's face was aglow. "And more! It's got to be worth a couple hundred thousand, right? So you can get caught up with the bills, maybe even put some money away for next year."

Nate appeared over Frankie's shoulder. Just in time to catch her as her legs went out and she fainted, dead as a mackerel.

Chapter Sixteen

When Frankie came around, she was in Nate's arms in the kitchen. Alex, Joy and George were staring at her.

"Guess she isn't used to good news," George said as he chewed on a cookie.

"I'm okay," she murmured, pushing against Nate's chest.

He put a glass of orange juice in front of her. "Drink this."

"No, I'm really okay." She got to her feet, amused to find the ring clutched in her hand. Even when she'd been unconscious, she'd known enough not to lose the thing.

As she looked at the diamond, she thought, so this was what winning the lottery felt like. It was good. Really, really damn good.

"Isn't this just amazing!" Joy exclaimed.

"You'll have better luck selling it down in the city,"

Nate said. "I've got some friends in the diamond district who can take care of it for you."

Frankie nodded. "But let's find out what it's worth, first. I'll take it to Albany tomorrow. To the jeweler who sold Grand-Em's other rings."

There was a pause. Everyone seemed to be waiting for her to say something.

She smiled and then, suddenly, she couldn't stop beaming. "You know what we need to do? Let's go out to dinner. To celebrate. Let's get Grand-Em and go to the Silver Diner and eat ourselves silly."

"Me, too?" George asked.

"Of course!" Frankie started laughing and pumped the ring over her head. "Let's hear it for salvation."

There was a hearty cheer from the group and even Alex cracked a smile.

In the end, her brother elected to stay behind, but Grand-Em was thrilled with the invitation. The five of them were just leaving the house when the phone started to ring. Frankie paused, hand on the back door.

"Let it go to voice mail," Nate said in her ear. "All the guests are accounted for. And we'll only be gone for an hour."

But she couldn't do it. After a decade of being tied to the phone, letting it go knowingly unanswered felt like child abandonment.

She was breathless from rushing to her desk as she picked up. She recognized the voice instantly and felt a sliver of dread.

"Nate," she called out. "It's for you. Spike."

Nate frowned and strode through the kitchen to the office.

"What's doing?" he said into the receiver.

"I've found the joint, man. It's perfect. In the theater district. We went there to eat just a couple of months ago. Tamale's."

Nate propped his hip against the desk. He knew the place. It was small, intimate. Kitchen was open to the dining area. Nice area of the city to be in. "Why are the owners selling?"

"Well, that's the thing. They're not sure they want to, but they're getting spanked. Tex-Mex is passé so they're not covering food and labor costs and their head chef quit two days ago when he got raided by someone else. The owners called me, wondering if I'd take over the stove. I went out for a drink with them last night, and man, they've got that bloody-eyeball exhaustion thing hanging around them like a funeral dirge. We got talking about their operation, and when I mentioned you and I were looking to buy, they were interested in getting together again. They seem desperate, so maybe they'll even hold paper for a while so we'll have a little more breathing room with the money. This is friggin' fantastic, man. Just what we've been looking for."

Nate frowned. "If they want to sell."

"That's where you come in, you Harvard-ass educated, fancy talkin' SOB. They're right on the edge and you're just the man to shoulder-check them into the abyss. Or have you forgotten your hockey moves?" Spike chuckled, but then his voice got serious. "Man, this has *got* to be it. We've been trying so damn hard and I'm tired of being on the sidelines. I have to get back to work, Walkman, I really do."

Nate could totally understand that. He'd been itchy as hell before he'd taken over at White Caps.

"So when're you coming down?" Spike demanded.

Nate thought about White Caps' kitchen. There wasn't much he could do, and now that Frankie had the ring, he felt less like he'd be abandoning her at a terrible time.

"Give me two days."

"Good deal." There was a pause. "We're going to make this work, Walkman. And we're going to have a friggin' blast doing it."

Nate hung up. And felt curiously numb.

He should be more psyched. Hell, he should be panting to get into Lucille and head down to the city. What was his problem?

Maybe it was because there wasn't really a deal, only the possibility of a deal. Maybe he'd just gotten his hopes up too many times.

Frankie poked her head in the door. "Everything okay?"

Or maybe it was something else entirely.

Nate drank in the sight of her. The light from overhead fell onto the dark waves of her hair and brought the features of her face out into high relief. She was wearing a little white shirt and a pair of well-worn jeans and had red flip-flops on her feet.

"Nate?"

He rubbed the middle of his chest. "Yeah. It's all good."

But was it? He heard the enthusiasm in Spike's voice again as well as the man's desperation to get back to the job he loved. He and Spike had made a pact to find their fortune together. Spike was relying on him to keep up his side of the bargain.

Good God, Nate thought, wrenching a hand through his hair. Was he actually considering pulling out?

Panic swirled in his gut.

No. He wasn't.

He was a man of his word. And besides, being an owner was his dream, too. He wasn't doing it as a favor to Spike.

"Nate?" she whispered.

He forced a smile and pushed himself off the desk.

"Come on, let's go." He put his arm around her shoulders and kissed her.

"He found something, didn't he."

Nate stared down into her eyes. "Yes, he did."

As everyone piled into the Honda and Frankie got behind the wheel, she was frustrated. Damn it, White Caps had just been saved and here she was, back in the doldrums. She needed to lighten up.

But how could she? The idea that Nate was going to the city in forty-eight hours to look at a place to buy made the end of the summer so real.

When they got to the Silver Diner, everyone was talking at the same time, George and Nate about sports, Joy and Grand-Em about some gala that had been held in 1954. Frankie felt herself withdrawing, just pinning a smile on her face and watching them all as if they were on TV.

Throughout dinner, she kept looking at Nate and finding herself missing him. When the meal was over and they filed out of the restaurant, he put his hand on the small of her back and guided her through the maze of tables in the back room and then past the stools in the rail car. His touch was firm, warm. Tantalizing.

How was she going to say goodbye?

God, their end was coming so fast, so soon. Whether

or not he bought the place Spike had called about or not, Labor Day was just a couple weeks away.

As if he sensed her thoughts, Nate massaged her shoulder. She covered his hand with hers, feeling the warmth of his skin. As they stepped out into the night air together, they let the others go ahead.

Frankie stopped walking and closed her eyes, trying to force the memory of the moment into her mind. The feel of his touch, the smell of him, the knowledge that they were going home and sharing the same bed tonight.

"I just want to hold on tight to this," she whispered.

He pressed his lips to her forehead. "Me, too."

When they got home, Frankie checked on Alex before going to her room. He didn't stir as she opened the door and she looked at the sample packs of Percocet his doctors had given him. He hadn't been taking the pills, which was a relief because that Scotch bottle was now empty.

God, he looked haggard even as he slept.

Frankie shut off the light on the bureau.

"Do you love him?" Alex asked in the darkness.

She gasped. "I didn't know you were awake."

"You think I can sleep?"

"You drank enough."

Alex cursed softly. "Not nearly."

Frankie walked over to the bed and sat down carefully on the edge. "Is there anything I can get you?"

"Stop asking me that, okay? It makes me feel like a cripple. Besides, what I want I can't have."

Frankie smiled sadly. She and Alex had always had quick tempers and she knew exactly how he was feeling right now. His skin was probably itching for her to leave him alone.

"Well, do you?" her brother demanded. "Love that guy?"

"I don't know." Actually, she did. But she couldn't say the words out loud.

"He's not bad, you know."

She laughed. "Now there's a ringing endorsement."

"I like the way he takes care of you."

"Me, too." She took a deep breath. "But he's leaving soon. Going back to New York. He's want to open his own restaurant."

"You going with him?"

"God, no. Who would run this place?"

"Then he should stay here with you." Alex's voice was biting with disapproval.

"He has a right to follow his dream."

"He's a fool."

She glared into the dark. "How can you of all people say that? You left Saranac because what you wanted couldn't be found here. Why can't he do the same?"

"Because you're my sister."

"And I was your sister back when Mom and Dad died, too. That didn't stop you then, did it?" She slapped her hand over her mouth. "I'm sorry, Alex. I didn't mean—"

"It's okay. I deserved that. And more."

They were silent for a while. He shifted on the bed and grunted.

"I'm so damn sorry about what happened," he said softly.

She put her hand on his arm. "But the Coast Guard said the accident wasn't your fault—"

"No, about you staying behind all those years ago and taking care of Joy and Grand-Em. I didn't give you a choice. I took off and left you to clean everything up and it wasn't fair. That's why I want Nate to stay. So someone can take care of you for a change."

Her breath caught.

"I want you to know something, Frankie. You did a great job raising Joy. Mom and Dad would have been so proud of you. Not surprised, just proud."

"Thank you," she whispered as she started to cry.

Alex cleared his throat as he moved his arm away from her touch. "Anyway."

She sniffled. "I'm so glad you said something. I—"

"You better go to your man, now. You should enjoy him while you have him," he said gruffly. "Although I still think he's a fool for leaving."

"Alex—"

"Go on. I'm tired."

She wiped her tears away and stood up. "Okay, I'm leaving."

As she shut the door, she thought that Alex was as Grand-Em had become. Every once in a while, you'd get a glimpse at what was inside.

But it never lasted long enough.

Late the following afternoon, Nate wiped plaster dust out of his eyes as he got off the stepladder and put down the crowbar. He'd finished removing the last of the water-damaged sections of Sheetrock from the rafters. With a clear path made, a fresh ceiling could be put up the minute those new pipes were installed.

"Excuse me, Chef?"

Nate turned around and looked at Henry. The boy was with his mother and dressed in real clothes, not the bathing suit and life jacket that had been his uniform of late.

"Hey, bud. What's up?"

Since their conversation on the dock, the kid had managed to corner him two more times. They'd covered vegetables while on a tour of Frankie's garden and then bread-making.

"We're leaving." Henry marched forward, holding out an envelope. "I wanted to give this to you so you could remember me. We're coming next year, and even though your kitchen's ruined now, I want to see you when I come back so we can sit on the dock again. Because you never did finish telling me about chickens, you know, and I really should know about them if I'm going to go to cooking school like you did and wear a big tall hat…"

Nate took the envelope and glanced at the boy's mother. She smiled and mouthed the words, *thank you for being his friend.*

"…and my dad said it's only about three hundred miles to the city so you could come visit us if you wanted to…"

As the chatter continued, Nate realized he was going to miss the kid.

"…and that's all I have to say about that." Henry put his hands on his hips. "So can I have a hug now?"

Nate swallowed. And then carefully put the envelope on the counter. He knelt down and opened his arms, not sure what to expect. Henry, however, was an old hat at the hug thing. He launched himself like a bottle rocket into the chest that was being offered and grabbed onto Nate's neck so hard Nate saw stars.

Henry pulled back. "See you next summer."

And then he marched over to his mother, took her hand, and led her out the door.

Nate let himself fall back onto the floor.

A moment later, he reached up for the envelope. Inside was a black-and-white photograph of Henry and him in the garden. Nate was pointing over the boy's shoulder to a tomato plant and Henry was looking up gravely. One of Henry's parents must have taken it, though Nate had never noticed because keeping up with that kid required a lot of concentration.

After staring at the image for a long time, Nate took the picture and put it to his chest.

In the distance, he heard the phone ring and Frankie's voice as she picked up in her office. She'd just returned from Albany. The gemologist had been out that morning, but the jeweler's assistant had promised her an answer from the man soon.

"Nate! It's for you."

He put the picture back into the envelope so it was safe and went to her office. After giving her a quick kiss on the mouth, he picked up the receiver.

Spike got right to the point. "Change in plan, Walkman. Evidently, I talked Tamale's owners into selling on my own. They're putting the place on the market tomorrow at noon and I'm at our lawyer's right now. What did the bank say we could do, outside limit?"

Nate rattled off the numbers for a down payment and final purchase price, knowing them by heart. As he talked, he was aware that Frankie was scribbling on a sheet of paper, trying to look disinterested.

When he was finished, Spike read the figures back. "Do I have this right?"

"Wait," Nate blurted.

"What did I screw up?"

There was a tense silence. Nate had a sour taste in his mouth, like he'd chewed tin. His stomach was on fire.

"Nate? What's the problem?" When he didn't answer, Spike's voice grew frustrated. "What's going on?
This is exactly what we've been waiting for and the
damn thing's going to go fast. I'll fax the papers to you
so you can review and sign them and then first thing tomorrow our lawyer's going to put the bid in. We need
to be on the ball here."

"I know." So why did he feel deflated?

"Are we going to do this thing or what?"

Nate forced himself to speak. "Yeah. Let's do it."

He hung up and found himself staring at Frankie's
hand as it gripped the pen she'd been moving in aimless circles. Her knuckles were white.

"I hope you get the place," she said brightly as she
looked up. "I know you're going to be a huge success."

But her eyes didn't meet his. They were focused
over his shoulder, and when he glanced behind him, he
saw what she was looking at.

It was the picture of her family together, taken all
those years ago.

Frankie snuck out of the house an hour later. Nate
was busy getting faxes off the machine and reviewing
his offer. He'd looked up when she told him she was
going out. He'd wanted to know where she was headed
and she told him she wasn't sure, she'd just wanted
some air.

Except she knew exactly where she was going. And
she wanted to go there alone.

She crossed Route 22 and walked into the woods,
picking up the dirt road. When the trailhead appeared
to the left, she stayed in her tire groove as it curved in
the opposite direction. When the cemetery's entrance

appeared, she faltered briefly, the sight of all the grave-stones chilling her. But she forced herself to keep going, stepping forward and walking around the gate. Inside, the grass under foot was long, ready for a mowing.

Her parents' headstones were over to the left and she went to them slowly. Joy's flowers had long wilted and the pink taffeta bow had collapsed in on itself. Frankie picked up the bouquet, stripped off the bow and tossed the dead flowers into the bushes.

While she tucked the ribbon into her pocket, she read the inscription on her father's marker. It was a relief to find she didn't feel like screaming at him. She was sad and she missed him, but she was too distraught to yell.

Nate was leaving, her heart was breaking, and what she was looking for from the slate headstones, what she wanted from the cool quiet of the place, was peace. Peace with her decision to stay when part of her wanted to go. Peace with the sacrifice she was making.

She looked at her mother's stone and reached down to brush off some of the memorial hemlock's needles from the top.

Maybe she'd also come up because of what Alex had said to her the night before. The idea that her parents would have been proud of her was a balm of sorts. And Alex, though he didn't say a lot, always spoke the truth.

Before she knew what she was doing, she sat down in the grass and leaned back against the hemlock. Its trunk was strong, supporting her weight easily while she stared at her parents' graves.

She took deep breaths in spite of the ache in her heart. And after a while, a kind of calm came. There would be no peace, she realized. Not without Nate in her life. But there was relief to be had that White Caps was safe for at least another year or two. Alex would be able to recover at home. Grand-Em would have the continuity with her past that helped preserve what little of her sanity was left. And Joy wouldn't have to go out and get some office job to support herself. She could continue to design dresses and work with the fabrics she loved so much.

And as for her, Frankie thought. What would she have?

Her family.

They'd been enough for her before she'd known Nate. And they would have to suffice now, too. Because as much as she loved him, she couldn't give up her sister and her brother and her grandmother and her home and the place she loved to live in just for a man who was only "emotionally attached."

If he'd loved her, things might have been different.

But he'd never said the words and she wasn't about to ask. That was just too much like begging for her to stomach.

Besides, if you had to pose the question, chances were you weren't going to like the answer.

The next morning, Nate woke up alone. He'd overslept after having tossed and turned for most of the night. The bid that he and Spike had put together was a good one and he should have been thrilled. But triumph was not what had kept him up.

He swung his legs over the side of the mattress and looked out at the water. It was another crystal clear day, an early harbinger of fall's arrival. Looking at the cloudless blue sky, he thought of Frankie saying that she'd found herself in the seasons of Saranac Lake.

He could see why.

When he went downstairs, he looked for her and found her in her office. She smiled at him, but her eyes were vacant. This was not a surprise. Ever since the call from Spike had come in yesterday, she'd been pulling away by inches and then feet. She'd even stayed on her side of the bed last night.

"Hey," he said, leaning against the doorjamb.

She shuffled some papers. "Good morning. How did you sleep?"

Her tone was flat, as if he were a guest.

"Badly." He stepped into the room. He wanted to talk with her about when she'd come down to the city to visit in September, when he could come back to White Caps.

As if by making plans, he could keep them together.

"Listen, Frankie—"

The phone rang and she answered in that same pleasant monotone. But then her voice grew tense. "Mr. Robinson, thanks for getting back to me so fast. What's the ring worth?"

Nate scanned her face, hoping it was a big number. A huge number. A number that would keep her house safe. Take some of the pressure off of her. Make her happy.

But her mouth sagged and her eyes blinked rapidly.

A sickening jolt went through him.

"You're kidding me," she whispered. "No, no, I trust you. I do. You were always fair to us before. Yeah, I'll come by and pick it up. Actually, could you just mail it to me?"

When she put the receiver down, her skin was the color of fog.

"Paste," she murmured. "The ring is paste. Worth maybe a hundred bucks."

Nate cursed under his breath.

The sound of his voice seemed to energize her and she leaped to her feet, throwing her chair back. Her body began to shake, her eyes going opaque with frustrated agony. She looked down, breath coming out in short bursts as her emotions surged.

There was a long silence so tense, he thought he was going to have to scream for her.

But then with a violent heave, she pushed everything off the top of her desk. Just swept it clean with her arms. The phone and the pens and pencils, the pads of paper and the files, it all hit the floor in a loud clatter. She started crying in great heaves, making guttural noises that were nothing like words. Wheeling around, she looked with wild eyes at the room as if searching for something else to destroy. And then she threw herself upon her bookshelves with a vengeance. She tore at them with clawlike hands, ripping the volumes out, slinging them behind her.

He didn't try and stop her. Instead, he quickly shut the door to the office and braced his back against it, in case anyone tried to get in. He knew exactly how she felt. When he'd learned about what Celia had done to their child, he'd trashed his whole apartment.

But Frankie didn't take it that far.

Moments later, she collapsed on the floor, in the middle of the mess she'd made. She was crippled by wave upon wave of the dry heaves, falling on to her side, her tears streaming down as her body spasmed.

That was when he went to her. He gathered her close, but held her loosely because he didn't want her to feel trapped.

As he held her sobbing body, he realized he couldn't leave her.

Not for the dreams he'd held for so long. Not for Spike. Not for the promise of independence and respect.

God, he loved her. He *loved* her. Loved her like no other. And life without her, even in the glamorous world of New York City, was going to be pale and uninteresting and worthless.

He smoothed her hair back from her face.

And realized he had the power to do what the ring couldn't. He had the money to save her house.

Keeping her against his chest, he dragged the phone over. He had to work to get a dial tone, but eventually one came and when Spike answered his cell phone, relief hit Nate like a linebacker.

"I can't do it, Spike. I'm sorry man, I can't do it. I can't put that offer in."

Frankie stiffened against him.

"What the hell are you talking about?" his friend demanded.

"I'm sorry. I've got…another thing I have to do."

Frankie pulled away, wiping her eyes with her sleeve. "What are you doing?" she croaked.

Spike was equally shocked. "You can't be serious—"

"What are you doing?" Frankie repeated, voice getting stronger. "I'm not going to let you—"

"What the hell are you saying, Walker!"

Nate gave them both a chance to yell at him. And then he took control of the situation.

"Let me call you back, Spike." He hung up and held onto Frankie as she tried to stand up. "I can help you, Frankie. The money I have will—"

"No! I don't want your charity," she said.

He grinned. Such a damn fighter. "Then how about we go into business together? Partners."

She shook her head, still trying to get away from him. "No. No way. You're going to end up hating it here. You're going to resent me and this house and everything you've given up."

"Since when can you see into the future?"

"Nate, I'm not going to let you do this. Just because you feel badly for me—"

"Shut up." He kissed her. "I love you. That's why I'm doing it."

She blinked at him, as if he'd spoken in a foreign language. "You what?"

"I. Love. You." God, his heart felt lighter than it had in years. It was positively singing in his chest. "I love you. I *love* you. I love *you*. You know, those three words have quite a ring to them."

Frankie shook her head. "But what about your dreams? You're giving them up."

"Naw. Just changing their address. And I'll talk to Spike. I don't think he cares where we are as long as we're working."

When she just stared at him, he felt a moment's panic. What if she didn't love him back?

Nate stroked her cheek with his thumb, tension tightening his shoulders. "Say something. Frankie? Will you please…just say something."

"I love you, too," she blurted.

He closed his eyes. "God, I was hoping—"

"But you're crazy! To give up—"

Nate kissed her long and hard, pushing her back down against the floor in the mess of papers. He'd meant only to quiet her, but the passion took over and soon she was moaning and he was nudging her legs apart. As he settled against her body, he found her breast with his hand.

His voice was hoarse as he whispered into her throat. "And exactly how do you think I'm giving up anything? When we have this?"

Her hands came up and covered her eyes. "I hope I don't wake up now. I hope this is actually happening."

"I want to marry you."

She dropped her hands to the floor and laughed. "I *really* hope this isn't a dream."

"I'm serious."

Frankie looked up at him. Her eyes were full of tears again, but instead of pain, they were glowing with love. She reached out and touched his face.

"Truly?" she said, as if afraid to believe it.

"I want you to be my wife. Right now, as a matter of fact. You know a justice of the peace?"

She smiled. "Actually I think the plumber's one in his spare time. And given the number of hours he's spent here lately…"

"So we're engaged?"

She wrapped her arms around him, pulling his head down. "Yeah, we're engaged."

"Good." He mouth found hers, but he was gentle this time. "I love you. God, I just want to keep saying that."

She broke the sweet contact. "Nate?"

"Hmm?"

"I know who I want to be my bridesmaid."

"Joy will be thrilled."

"Well, yes, but I want another one." She laughed. "I want Lucille to be at our wedding. Because if she hadn't broken down, you never would have walked through my back door."

Nate grinned, feeling as if everything in his life had fallen into place. "You know something? That car's going to look wonderful in a taffeta skirt."

* * * * *

*Don't miss Jessica Bird's next visits
with the Moorehouse family.
Look for Joy's story and Alex's story in 2006.
Only from Silhouette Special Edition!*

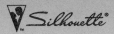

SPECIAL EDITION™

At last!

From *New York Times* bestselling author

DEBBIE MACOMBER

comes

NAVY HUSBAND

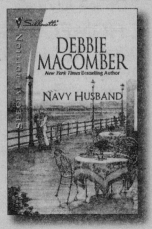

**This is the final book in her beloved Navy series—
a book readers have requested for years.**

The Navy series began in Special Edition in 1988
and now ends there with *Navy Husband*,
as Debbie makes a guest appearance.

*Navy Husband is available from
Silhouette Special Edition in July 2005.*

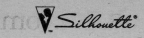

SPECIAL EDITION™

presents a new six-book continuity

MOST LIKELY TO...

**Eleven students. One reunion.
And a secret that will change everyone's lives.**

On sale July 2005

THE HOMECOMING HERO RETURNS

(SE #1694)

by bestselling author

Joan Elliott Pickart

Former college jock David Westport was convinced he had it all—a beautiful wife, two wonderful kids and a good business in his North End neighborhood. Sandra Westport loved her husband dearly but was positive that he did have one regret—letting her sudden pregnancy derail his chances at a pro baseball career ten years ago. And when a college professor revealed a secret that threw all the good in David's life into shadow, Sandra feared her marriage was over. Could David rebuild his shattered dreams without losing the love of his life?

Don't miss this emotional story—only from Silhouette Books.

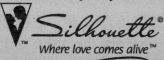

Where love comes alive™

SSETHHR

If you enjoyed what you just read,
then we've got an offer you can't resist!

Take 2 bestselling love stories FREE!

Plus get a FREE surprise gift!

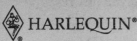

HARLEQUIN®

NeXt™

Every Life
Has More Than
One Chapter.

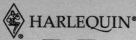

HARLEQUIN®

NExt™

**Every Life
Has More Than
One Chapter.**

Receive $1.00 off

your Harlequin NEXT™ novel.

**Four titles available each month,
beginning July 2005.**

Coupon expires October 31, 2005.
Redeemable at participating retail outlets
in the U.S. only. Limit one coupon per customer.

OFFER 11171

5 65373 00076 2 (8100) 0 11171